D0209645

THE FOURTH NEPHITE

THE FOURTH NEPHITE

JEFFREY S. SAVAGE

DESERET
BOOK

SALT LAKE CITY, UTAH

Library of Congress Cataloging-in-Publication Data
Savage, Jeffrey S., 1963–
    The fourth Nephite / Jeffrey S. Savage.
        p. cm. — (The fourth Nephite ; bk. 1)
    Summary: When he jeopardizes his football scholarship, high school student Kaleo is transported from present-day Salt Lake City to early nineteenth-century Palmyra, New York, where he meets the Prophet Joseph Smith and learns for himself the truthfulness of the Book of Mormon.
    ISBN 978-1-60641-657-0 (paperbound) 4360 6424 10/10
    [1. Mormons—Fiction. 2. Smith, Joseph, 1805–1844—Fiction. 3. Time travel—Fiction.] I. Title. II. Series: Savage, Jeffrey S., 1963– Fourth Nephite ; bk. 1.
    PZ7.S259Fo 2010
    [Fic]—dc22   2010015662

Printed in the United States of America
Publishers Printing, Salt Lake City, UT

10 9 8 7 6 5 4 3 2 1

To my son Scott Allen Savage,
who, at the time of this writing,
is serving in the Ohio Columbus Mission.

And to my daughter, Erica Lyn Thurman,
who was recently sealed to the love of her life.

Thanks for surviving my parenting skills.

ACKNOWLEDGMENTS

Thanks to Chris Schoebinger for suggesting the idea for this series to me over lunch, even though it wasn't what I had come to hear.

Thanks to James Dashner for giving me the title over Mexican food. (What is it with writing and lunch?)

Thanks to Lisa Mangum for her wonderful insights and editing, Owen Richardson for the great cover, and all the others at Deseret Book for making this work possible.

A special thanks to Kathy and Tyler Clement, Dick and Vicki Savage, Riley Lewis, my awesome critique group, and the many others who read this book in its earliest stages and gave me great feedback, and to Mark Namba who helped me with football insights. Thanks to Copper Hills High School for letting me use your team name, even though I modified the school colors for artistic purposes.

To my amazing wife, Jennifer, who is my best friend and best reader, and to my four awesome kids—thanks for understanding when I disappear for hours at a time into my office.

And most of all, thanks to the great men and women who sacrificed so much so the gospel of Jesus Christ could be restored to the earth in its fullness.

There are different levels of uncoolness. Refusing to share the wealth when your mom sends fresh chocolate chip cookies in your lunch is a three. Snaking your friend's girl away from him is a seven—but a five if she's totally hot and they're only going out because his dad bought him a Mustang for his sixteenth birthday. Not giving everything you've got on the football field is a nine. Getting caught with a beer in your hand by your seminary teacher the day before the regional championship game is off the charts.

Today I became the king of uncool.

CHAPTER 1

F riday's after-school practice was less than an hour—
mostly film recap of Freedom High's last two games
and a brief review of a couple of trick plays we might
have to use if Saturday's score was tight. We'd only lost one
game all year, and even that was on a last-second defensive
lapse. The Eagles were tough, but if we got past them, West
was supposed to be a piece of cake. Coach wouldn't say it, but
I knew his mind was on a state championship.

Walking from the locker room out to the snow-covered
parking lot, *my* mind was on the scouts from Michigan and
UCLA who were going to be at the game. I was pretty amped
up. Technically, the scouts were there to see both teams, but
both schools had asked me to sign a letter of intent, even
though I was still a junior. If I played well tomorrow I could
count on a full-ride scholarship to either of them.

"Steele," a voice called as I stepped into the icy air. A hand
big enough to smash my skull dropped onto my shoulder.

Have you ever seen a rhinoceros up close in a zoo? It's like standing face to face with Mother Nature's version of a Sherman tank. Even though the animal is locked safely behind bars, you get the feeling that if it decided to throw all five thousand pounds of armored muscle at the cage, nothing could stop it from trampling you flat.

"Crush" Carlton was Copper Hills High's rhino—two hundred and eighty pounds of pure nasty. His blocking was half the reason Jeff Greene, our senior quarterback, had connected with me for nearly three touchdowns a game this season. He'd also managed to send five defensive linemen off the field with assorted injuries.

"Careful where you put that thing," I said, mostly joking as he squeezed my arm.

"Only on the Eagles," Crush said, smacking a beefy fist into his palm with a grin that made me glad I was on his side of the line. His breath plumed in the cold air. "A few of us are going to have a little party. Get psyched up before the game. You in?"

I shook my head. "Sorry, bro. No can do. I want to get to bed early tonight." Living in Utah, most of the guys on the team were Mormon, and a lot of them harassed me about not planning on a mission. Crush was one of the few guys who didn't seem to care one way or the other. I liked that about him, but his "parties" often got a little crazy, and the last thing I needed was to get in trouble the night before the game of my life.

"Figured you'd say that." His eyes gleamed. "You really think Michigan's gonna be at the game?"

"That's what the rumor is." I played it cool, not admitting I knew it for a fact, because the scouts for both Michigan and UCLA had let me know personally that they'd be watching me.

"Man, what I wouldn't give to play for a school like that," Crush said. He was a brute on the field, but kind of a head case everywhere else. More than likely he'd end up with a smaller college or maybe a JC unless he cleaned up his act.

"Plant their nose guard into the turf a couple of times, and who knows?" I said.

"Yeah . . ." He gazed out at the field—cleared of snow and ready for the game—and I took the chance to jog toward my car, hoping he'd forget why he'd started talking with me in the first place.

No such luck.

"About the party," he said before I got more than a few steps away. "Knew you and Greene wouldn't want to stay up late, so guess what?"

I shook my head, knowing I wouldn't like whatever he had to say.

"We're having it right here—behind the bleachers on the other side of the field."

Behind the bleachers. I knew what kind of party that meant. Someone had talked an adult into buying them beers. Probably cigars too. Crush's idea of luxury was a cold beer in his hand and a cheap cigar stuck in his mouth—although I'd never actually seen him smoking. "Sorry, dude. My mom will kill me if I don't come straight home," I said. It was the truth.

"Come on, man." He caught up with me, leaned close to my ear, and whispered, "We invited some of the cheerleaders. But they won't come unless you and Greene are there."

"Greene's going?" I asked, turning around. Jeff Greene was Mormon too. In my ward, in fact. Although neither of us was what you'd call very active. We occasionally cut out of Sunday School when our parents weren't watching and went for doughnuts. As far as I knew, Jeff wasn't any more of a partier than I was, so I was surprised to hear he was coming.

"Sure." Crush beamed. "Told him it wouldn't be right for the star quarterback to dis the guys who are keeping him in one piece tomorrow."

That changed things a little. I could get by with blowing off Crush and whatever other guys he dragged with him. They'd probably get so drunk they wouldn't remember whether I'd been there or not. But Greene was my bread and butter. If *he* was going, I should at least stop by.

"You're *sure* Jeff will be there?"

Crush grinned again, knowing he had me. "Kaleo, my man, would I lie to the guy who's going to take us to state?"

The next thing I knew, I was heading reluctantly across the field with Crush and a few of his buddies. Sure enough, I spotted Greene a few yards away—although he didn't look any more excited than I. It was probably the cheerleaders that did it. I hadn't heard of Jeff drinking, but he was definitely a ladies' man.

I glanced back over my shoulder, hoping the rest of the team hadn't seen where I was headed. That was another thing about living in Utah. Most of the other guys on the team were good Mormons—going to seminary, reading their scriptures, planning on serving missions. The last thing I needed was for them to spot me hanging out with guys like Crush.

"Surprised to see you partying the day before you make the college scouts true believers," Jeff said as we crossed the fifty-yard line.

"Same with you," I said. Greene and I were both hoping to make it to the pros one day—him with his arm, and me with my speed and hands. We were tight on the field and friends off of it, but that didn't keep us from being competitive every chance we got.

"Wasn't going to," Jeff grinned. "How could I say no when Crush told me you were coming to support the line?"

"Wait, he told you . . . ?" I looked at Crush and his buds—who all had suspicious lumps hidden beneath their letterman jackets—and kicked at a clump of ice that somehow hadn't been cleared. "I think we've been set up."

By then we'd reached the bleachers. Someone had cleared the snow from a patch of winter-brown grass out of sight of the school and the parking lot. A bunch of five-gallon buckets turned upside down provided chairs, and just as Crush had said, a handful of varsity cheerleaders were standing around nervously, hands tucked in their jacket pockets.

Despite the cold, they were all wearing their cheer outfits. I never understood how they stayed warm in those skirts.

Maybe they were just a lot tougher than us jocks. I'd be complaining up a storm if I had to stand around in something like that with the snow blowing up off the cold field.

"Hey guys!" a cute senior with long blonde hair squealed.

"She's talking to you, Kaleo," Greene said, elbowing me in the ribs.

I shook my head. *He* was the babe magnet. I liked girls just fine, and as a football player I'd had plenty of chances to go out on dates. But being raised in a house full of boys, I'd never had a sister to teach me how to act around girls. "All yours," I said, wondering why I was even there.

Jamming my hands into my jacket, I found an empty bucket and sat down. Somebody threw a couple pieces of wood into a cut-off metal barrel that reminded me of the ones we used at Scout camp, and got a smoky fire going. I should have known Crush was working me. Now I just had to figure out how quickly I could make my escape without anyone noticing.

"Mind if I sit with you?" asked a soft voice. It was the girl who'd said hi earlier. I thought her name was Tanya or Tammy, something that started with a T. She looked cold—and yeah, kind of cute too.

Immediately my heart began beating way too fast, and my mouth went dry. "Sure, I guess," I mumbled, wondering how we were both going to balance on the top of a five-gallon bucket.

That turned out not to be a problem. She plopped onto my knees with a grin. Why is it that I can face a two-hundred pound defensive back with no problem, but the minute I find myself face to face with a hundred pound girl, my entire body breaks into an icy sweat? It didn't help that she leaned against me, her head almost resting on my shoulder.

As usual, I found myself sitting silently with absolutely no idea what to say. The more I tried to think of something interesting, the more stupid I sounded inside my head. The only thing that saved me from making a total fool of myself was Crush showing up with his arms around a pair of cheerleaders. Clearly he had no problem talking to girls.

"Looks like you and Terri are getting comfortable," he said.

Terri, I reminded myself.

"Got something for you two," Crush said. A huge brown cigar jutted from the corner of his mouth, bouncing up and down as he spoke. I'm sure he thought it made him look cool, but to me he looked like a total flake. Taking his arm from around one of the girls, he slipped a hand into his jacket and pulled out a couple of beer bottles from an inside pocket. "To a total beat down of the Eagles tomorrow."

Before I could tell Crush I wasn't drinking, Terri took the bottles. "Cheers," she said with a toothy grin. One at a time, she twisted open the tops. Taking a swallow from one of the bottles, she held the other out to me.

I'd like to say I turned her down. That I realized I was crazy for coming to Crush's party in the first place, left Terri with the rest of the group, and went back to my car. That ten minutes later I was safe at home reading over my playbook and smelling the aroma of roasting pork for the feast my mom served after every game.

But that didn't happen. Maybe it was the way Terri's deep green eyes messed with my head. Maybe it was the way no one else seemed to have a problem with what they were doing. I could swear my mind was saying no, but somehow my hand ended up taking the bottle.

Would I have joined the rest of them in drinking and joking? I'll probably never know, because at that moment everyone went absolutely silent. All heads turned toward the end of the bleachers where a man in a dark suit and a long gray coat was watching us. There were at least a dozen kids around me, but the man's eyes went straight to mine with laser beam accuracy. I felt all the blood leave my face.

It was my seminary teacher.

The first thing I felt seeing Brother Mortensen standing in the gloom of the bleachers was embarrassment. I wanted to sink into the ground and stay there forever. The second thing was denial. I hadn't meant to come here. I didn't actually drink anything. It was just a dumb mistake. Then I realized what this could mean to my coach, my team, my chance to impress the college scouts. Finally it occurred to me I'd have to explain to my mom what I'd been doing. That's when embarrassment and denial turned to total, all-out panic.

CHAPTER 2

I jumped to my feet, and Terri bounced off my knee with a surprised squeak. The beer in my hand fell to the snow-covered ground and foamed. Around me kids ran—shoving bottles inside their coats as they disappeared in all directions. I looked briefly for Jeff, but he was nowhere in sight. Had he spotted Brother Mortensen coming or had he left the party before things even got started?

Terri shrugged apologetically and took off with her friends. I wanted to run too. But I couldn't. The pain and disappointment on my teacher's normally upbeat face froze me in place.

"I-It's not . . ." I stammered, trying to think my way out of this mess. "I mean, I didn't . . ." My lips were ice-cold, and my tongue felt attached to the roof of my mouth.

Brother Mortensen shook his head and sighed. Without a word, he turned and began walking back across the field.

Instantly my paralysis broke. "Hey, wait up," I yelled, racing after him. "I know what this looks like, but I swear I didn't drink anything."

He wouldn't look at me. Instead he marched steadily across the frozen turf, his head down, his blue-and-gray scarf blowing in the cold wind. I wanted to reach out and grab him, but something stopped me. We were studying the Book of Mormon that year. In one of the few classes where I'd paid attention, we learned about how Nephi shocked his brothers when they tried to lay their hands on him. I knew I wouldn't get shocked if I touched my seminary teacher, but looking at his grim expression, I felt that way.

"Please," I begged, seeing my successful football season disappearing with one stupid mistake. "Don't tell anyone. I swear I'll never do anything like this again."

At last he stopped. He still wouldn't look at me though. His gaze was glued to the ground in front of him. I expected him to say something, but his lips pressed tightly together.

Bouncing from one foot to the other, I waited for him to break his silence.

"Okay," I said at last, unable to stand the quiet. "I screwed up. I admit that. But if you tell anyone I had a beer on school property, it's an automatic ten-day suspension. I'll miss tomorrow's game."

Brother Mortensen blew out a long, slow breath. "Is that all you're worried about?" he asked softly. "Missing a football game?"

"This isn't just *any* football game. It's *region*. There are going to be college scouts there. If I miss it, I could ruin my chance for a scholarship." I clenched and unclenched my fists. "I know that doesn't mean much to you, but it's what I've been working for my whole life."

He nodded slowly, still not meeting my eyes. "So . . . you want me to forget what I saw?"

Maybe he understood after all.

"To lie?" he continued, and my relief disappeared.

I knew I couldn't ask him to lie. And I got the feeling he considered not telling anyone the same thing as lying. "Could you at least wait until after tomorrow's game?" I'd still get suspended and miss playing for the state championship—and I didn't even want to think about what my mom would do to me—but I'd least I'd get to play in front of the scouts.

For the first time, Brother Mortensen looked at me. His gray eyes stared so hard, I wanted to look away, but I made myself meet his gaze. "Who *are* you?" he asked.

I blinked. "I'm in your class. You know who I am."

"No." He shook his head and tucked his scarf into his coat. I could see the worn quad he took with him everywhere sticking out from the leather case he held. "I *thought* I knew you. You've made some mistakes, like we all do. But I always thought you had a working moral compass inside—a personal Liahona. Now I'm not so sure."

I felt my cheeks heat at his words. I've got a little problem with my temper. You'd think it would have come from my dad's side of the family. He's Scots-Irish, which should make him a hothead, but my dad is probably the calmest guy I've ever met in my life. My mom, who was born and raised on the Hawaiian island of Lanai, which is a very quiet and laid-back place, is another story. You don't want to mess with her.

"You think I'm a bad person because I took a beer?"

"It doesn't matter what I think." Brother Mortensen's lips rose in a tight smile and for a second I thought he was mocking me. My hands balled into fists. Then he took out his scriptures. "It matters what *you* think."

"*I* think I wasn't the only one at the party," I said, knowing how lame that sounded, but not caring.

"I'm not worried about them right now. I'm worried about you." He flipped through pages covered with colored highlights until he found what he was looking for. "Matthew 6:24," he said. "Do you remember it?"

It sounded vaguely familiar. Like maybe it was a Scripture Mastery verse or something. He handed me the book. Scowling, I found the passage. "'No man can serve two masters: for either he will hate the one, and love the other; or else he will hold to the one, and despise the other. Ye cannot serve God and mammon,'" I read, my nose growing numb. "So?"

Brother Mortensen took back his scriptures and tucked them into his case. "So you're straddling the fence right now— trying to keep one foot on both sides. I've been hoping that you'd come around eventually and remember who you are."

I stomped my freezing feet, trying to get the blood flowing. "What if I like who I am? I'm not a bad person just because I want to play football instead of going on a mission. Can I help it if I don't have my nose buried in the scriptures all the time?"

Something seemed to light up like a spark in the back of

Brother Mortensen's eyes—as if an idea had just occurred to him. "Have you read the Book of Mormon?" he asked.

"Some," I said, not wanting to admit I'd never gotten past the first few chapters of First Nephi.

"Do you believe it is the word of God?"

This whole thing felt like a Sunday School lesson. I knew I should say yes. That was obviously what he wanted to hear. But he was right about me. I was standing on both sides of the fence, and suddenly I was sick of pretending. "The word of God?" I shouted in his face. "More like the word of some kid with a crazy imagination. How can you take any of that seriously? Angels? Books made out of gold? Pillars of fire? It's all fantasy, just like *Lord of the Rings* or . . . or Harry Potter. But at least those authors admitted their books were stories."

I expected my teacher to explode. I knew he considered what I'd just said blasphemy. So I was confused when instead of shouting back at me, he smiled. "I'll make you a deal, Kaleo. I won't tell your coach or anyone else at school about what I saw today."

I waited for the inevitable *but*. When there was none, I shook my head. "What's the catch?"

"No catch. I won't tell anyone what I saw today. I'll leave it up to you whether you want to say anything or not."

"You're serious?" I was sure it had to be some kind of trap. But Brother Mortensen himself said that he didn't lie.

He opened his wallet and handed me a business card. I read the name on the front: Ladan. No last name—unless that *was* a last name. Below it was a Salt Lake address. The card looked old and wrinkled, as if Brother Mortensen had been carrying it around for a long time. I flipped it over. There was nothing on the back. "What is this?"

"The card is your part of the bargain," he said. "I agree not to say anything, and you agree to meet with this man."

"What is he, some kind of cop?" It couldn't be this easy. "Or is it someone from the Church?"

"Just a friend." Brother Mortensen put his wallet into his slacks. "He and I have known each other for quite a while. I think he might be able to help you."

"Help me what?" Maybe it was a trap after all.

"Ladan has a unique way of helping people see things more clearly. It's a little ironic when you think about it."

I had no idea what he was talking about, but the last thing I needed was a lecture from yet another preachy adult. Besides, the address was all the way downtown. My mom would skin me alive for driving into the city before a game. "Forget it."

Brother Mortensen nodded. "Fair enough. I'll just stop by the principal's office on the way back to my car."

Clenching the card between my fingers, I watched him turn and walk away. This was blackmail, plain and simple. The idea of having to listen to some guy preaching bored me to tears. But the idea of missing tomorrow's game was even worse. "Wait!" I called.

He stopped.

"What do I have to do?"

"Meet with Ladan." As he turned, I could see him trying to hide a smile, which ticked me off even more.

"That's all? I meet with him, and you agree not to tell?"

"That's all." He pinched his lip. "Of course, I will need proof that you actually met with him. How about if you have him write a note telling me that the two of you talked?"

If I could listen to my boring history teacher drone on and on about the politics of Colonial America without falling asleep, I could put up with anything. "I want your word. Promise me that if I bring back the note, you won't tell anyone, ever."

His hand dropped into his bag again, and I could imagine his fingers running across the pages of his scriptures, wanting to make me read more verses. Instead, he bobbed his head up and down once. "You talk to Ladan, and I won't say a thing. Of course if *you* decide to tell anyone, that's up to you."

I couldn't help laughing. Is that what this was about? He thought this Ladan dude would make me feel so guilty that I'd take myself out of the game? Apparently he didn't know who I was after all. "Deal."

He started to turn away, then glanced back over his shoulder. "Kaleo?"

"Yeah?" I asked, wondering if he was going to try to weasel out of our agreement.

"For what it's worth, I don't think you're a bad person."

Have you ever tried to find a parking space downtown on a Friday night? Moms who look like they teach Primary on Sundays suddenly become maniacs in SUVs. Old people cut across three lanes of traffic for an open meter. Minivans turn into torpedoes. It makes football seem like a non-contact sport.

CHAPTER 3

B y the time I finally found an open lot—six-freaking-
bucks for the first half-hour and five for every hour after that—it was almost six-thirty. I had called my mom
on the drive up and told her I was doing an assignment for
Brother Mortensen, which wasn't exactly a lie.

I think she was so shocked by the fact that I was doing
something related to seminary that she hardly argued at all.
She just told me to be home by eight. As I locked my car and
hurried out to the sidewalk, it was already dark. The cold air
ached in my lungs and froze my nostrils closed. I hoped it
would be a little warmer for the game tomorrow.

Thinking about the game, I glanced at the address on the
card again: 61 West South Temple. When Brother Mortensen
first sent me on this trip, I'd assumed I was going to a house.
But there were no residences around here. Nothing but office
buildings, construction sites where a new downtown was being

built, and—standing out brightly in the darkness—the Salt Lake Temple.

It was a week before Thanksgiving, and lots of people were out, shopping, sightseeing, or going to dinner. As I crossed Main Street, I realized the address was almost directly across from the south entrance of Temple Square. Dozens of families surged in and out of the gates, and more would be coming once the Christmas lights were turned on at Temple Square.

I remembered how cool it had been when I was little to come here with my parents. We made the drive every Christmas—looking at the lights, watching the live nativity, and following the spiral walkway up to the Christus statue. I looked forward to it for weeks. My family still came, but now I usually found an excuse to skip out on the trip. Somehow it just didn't feel the same anymore. Maybe I was too old for that kind of thing. Or maybe the magic had worn off.

Whatever the reason, I definitely wasn't here to see the temple now. In fact, the very sight of it reminded me of Brother Mortensen. Maybe the temple was another one of his tricks to make me feel guilty. If so, it wouldn't work. Turning my head away from the gleaming gray building, I searched for an address. The first building past the construction barriers was a tall office building. A gold 57 gleamed above the glass doors. The next building over had a sign for Utah Woolen Mills. Suits and expensive-looking ties hung in the window. It took me a minute find the address—59.

With my heart thudding, I passed the ramp that led to an underground parking garage and looked for the next building.

Just remember, I told myself, *whatever this guy says, don't argue. If he wants to preach, let him preach. Just get in and get out. And don't forget the note.*

On the other side of the garage, I stopped and found myself standing in front of a plywood wall painted white. Peeking through a crack in the wood, I could see the skeleton of a tall building being raised. A huge crane rose from the concrete and metal like the head of a dinosaur, but construction had stopped for the night and the site was deserted.

Realizing that couldn't be the address I was looking for, I hurried to the end of the barrier. When I reached it, I was standing at the corner of West Temple and South Temple. Across the intersection, I could see a JB's Restaurant, and past that, a hotel.

What was this? Some kind of joke? Slowly I made my way back toward the parking garage and the only buildings still standing—57, 59, and . . . nothing. I looked north across the street, but the entire block was taken up by Temple Square. I turned back the way I'd come, and seeing the blank white wall, felt a cold lump fill my stomach.

What if Brother Mortensen's card was outdated? What if the building this Ladan guy worked in had been torn down? Would Brother Mortensen believe me, or would he think I was just trying to get out of the deal? My legs started to tremble, and I let myself drop to the cold sidewalk. I tried to convince myself it was all a big joke—that my seminary teacher was just teaching me a lesson of some kind. But as hard as I tried,

I couldn't believe it. The whole thing was strange for sure, but Brother Mortensen was dead serious about it.

I considered trying to call him, to explain what had happened. But I didn't have his phone number. In fact I didn't even know exactly where he lived, or even his first name. He was just *Brother*. I could try forging a note, but my handwriting was so lousy I'd gotten caught the one time I tried faking an absent excuse from my mom.

For a second I considered saying a prayer. That's what I used to do when I lost things as a kid. But somehow I couldn't see myself praying for a way to get out of trouble for having a beer at school. And even if I could, I wasn't sure I believed anyone was listening to me.

As I sat on the curb, resting my head in my hands, something made a skittering noise behind me. Images of rats or stray dogs raced through my mind as I spun around. But the sidewalk was as empty as it had been before. Probably a leaf or a piece of trash blowing across the garage entrance . . . except the wind wasn't blowing.

I craned my neck around to search for what could have made the noise. Nothing in front of the office building. Nothing in front of the clothing store. The parking garage was dark and gated. There could be something farther down, but the noise had sounded closer. It sounded like it had come from right behind me. Right where that . . .

With my mouth hanging open, I stared into a narrow alleyway that I could swear hadn't been there a minute before. It was between the clothing store and the garage. I must have passed it twice. How could I have missed it? Unlike the rest of the block that was brightly lit, the alleyway was so dark I couldn't see more than a few feet inside.

Was that where the sound had come from? I wasn't so sure I wanted to go back there—even if a football game was riding on it.

"Hello?" I called, leaning toward the entrance. A man and woman walking along the sidewalk glanced briefly in my direction. The man shrugged his shoulders, and the woman laughed. Was she laughing at me? Suddenly I felt like a total dweeb. What was I so scared of? It was just an alley. So I'd missed it the first time—okay, the first *couple* of times. I'd been looking for a building, not some opening barely wide enough to squeeze into.

Shaking off my fear, I stood up, took a deep breath, and walked into the entrance. As soon as I stepped off the sidewalk, I saw the alley wasn't nearly as dark as it had looked from the street. With an almost full moon overhead and the light from the temple across the street, I could see the entire length of the alley. On one side was the concrete of the parking garage. On the other side was the brick wall of the clothing store. Halfway down the wall was a set of concrete steps leading up to a door. As I reached the steps, I saw a faded red 61 painted on the wall.

There was no sign or windows to give a hint as to what was inside. But I didn't care. I'd already wasted enough time. Without giving myself a chance to change my mind, I grabbed the doorknob and pushed. I was ready to face whatever was inside.

□   □   □

"Hello?" My voice echoed back at me as I leaned through the doorway.

The inside of the building was dimly lit by banks of flickering fluorescent bulbs thirty or forty feet overhead. The room was large and open like a warehouse, and much bigger than I'd expected.

The first thing I saw was a handcart. The kind they make you pull for youth conferences, so you can experience what the pioneers went through. Only this one looked old enough to have actually come across the plains. The wood was so dark and banged up, it looked like stone. The cart was filled with boxes, clothes, and pots.

Beside it, a dusty glass case had shelves of old coins and a collection of scissors and sewing needles.

This was so not what I'd expected.

"Hey," I called again, wondering if the place was closed for the night. "Is anyone here?"

The door swung shut behind me with a loud bang, and I nearly jumped out of my sneakers. This felt way too much like one of those horror movies where a bunch of zombies attack the poor guy who gets locked in an abandoned building at night.

The room looked a little like a museum with furniture, old tools, and piles of clothing stacked all around. But there were no signs or information on any of the exhibits. An antique store maybe? There were no price tags on the items or a cash register anywhere that I could see. My eyes went back to the coins again. They seemed pretty valuable. Who would leave the door of an antique store unlocked with no one to keep an eye on things?

I walked farther into the room, passing an old plow, a couple of wooden barrels, and a mannequin in a bonnet and a long dress, holding a tall wooden handle stuck into a barrel. As I stepped around the mannequin, it turned its head and looked straight at me.

"Geez!" I stumbled backward and fell against a pile of boxes. One of the boxes tipped over, spilling a bunch of buttons.

"Did I scare you?" the mannequin asked.

I put my hand over my heart, sure it was going to jump right out of my chest. Now that I was looking straight at her, I realized the mannequin was actually a girl my age, or maybe a little older. "No," I said, trying to catch my breath. "I always scream and nearly swallow my tongue when I meet new people."

The girl smiled. Even though I knew she was real, the old-fashioned clothes she was wearing still made her look a little like a pioneer exhibit. "Sorry," she said. "I should have said something when you came in."

"You think?" Gradually my pulse slowed back to normal. My elbow stung where I'd slammed it against the box of buttons. I looked down and saw that I'd scraped off a pretty good patch of skin. "What were you trying to do? Stop my heart?"

She laughed. It wasn't a mean laugh or teasing. Just amused. "I was actually a little surprised myself, or I would have spoken up. We don't get many customers here during the day, and no one comes at night."

"So, this is a *store?*" It was definitely the strangest one I'd ever seen.

She shrugged. "You could call it that I guess. We sell things. And sometimes we buy. But mostly we just rent."

Rent? I had no idea what she was talking about. Who would want to rent handcarts or old clothes or coins? Then it all made sense. "These are props, aren't they? Like for movies and stuff, right? None of it is real."

"Do you have any idea how much all this would be worth if it was authentic?" She tapped the barrel in front of her. "A butter churn in this kind of condition from the mid-seventeen-hundreds would be worth thousands of dollars. And that dough bin over there would be worth twice that."

"Seriously?" Who knew old stuff was worth so much? Most of it looked like it belonged in a thrift store to me. "So, are you an actress or something?" I asked, pointing to the bonnet the girl was wearing.

"Do I *look* like an actress?" she asked, narrowing her eyes as if she thought I was teasing her.

With her blonde curly hair and blue eyes, she could have been in movies. But she didn't seem to think so. Her face went red as she pulled off the bonnet and tucked it under one arm. "I work here. I just like putting on the clothes when no one's around. My great-great-great-grandmother's great-great-grandmother was one of the earliest members of the Church. It's fun to think about what it must have been like when she was a girl. Don't you ever wonder about what your ancestors were like?"

When she talked about her ancestors, the girl's face lit up. I had no idea how to respond to that. I knew my mother had joined the Church when she was a little girl, and I was pretty sure my dad's family had been members for at least a few generations. But I'd never really given it much thought before. At least not the way she seemed to have.

I looked around at all the old things, trying to see them from her point of view. All I could see was a bunch of stuff.

The girl leaned forward and took my arm. "You scraped that pretty good. Let's get you a bandage."

I knew she was trying to change the subject, but at the touch of her fingers, I suddenly realized I was standing there alone, talking to a good-looking girl. All at once, my mouth went dry, and I started to feel nervous.

"I really have to go," I said as she took to me to a cabinet and opened a first-aid kit. "I've got a big game tomorrow, and my parents will freak out if I don't get home soon."

She put the bandage on my elbow, then tilted her head to study me. "Why did you come here? Are you an actor?"

"Me?" Now I could feel *my* face getting hot. "No. I'm a football player. I had a . . . a . . . ." I pulled out the card and showed it to her. "I'm supposed to meet with Mr. Ladan."

"You're here to see *Ladan?*" Something crossed her face. I couldn't tell what it was. Amusement? Suspicion?

"My seminary teacher gave me this card. I had a sort of situation today." I swallowed, really not wanting to go into details. "Is he here? Will Mr. Ladan see me?"

She smiled slowly, and I wished I could read her thoughts. Did she know I'd gotten into trouble? Did a lot of kids get sent here to meet with Mr. Ladan?

"It's just Ladan," she said. "It's his first name. If he has a last name, he's never told it to me. And, yes, he's here. As far as whether he'll see you or not, you'll have to find that out for yourself." She pointed toward a door in the back corner of the room. It had an old-fashioned accordion-like metal gate across the front and there was a button next to it on the wall.

"An elevator?"

She nodded, still with that strange half-smile. "You've never been in the tunnels under the city, have you?"

"I didn't even know there were tunnels." This whole thing was getting way too strange. If it hadn't been for the football game, I'd have bailed on the spot—promise or no promise.

"There are miles of them. Pay close attention to the signs. You don't want to get lost down there."

Lost? What did she mean, "get lost?" As I pushed the button on the elevator and waited for it to clank and clang its way down to the basement, I imagined narrow passageways filled with steam pipes, rats, and maybe even a skeleton or two—kind of like the catacombs under the city of Paris I'd read about in school. If I hadn't been so stressed already it might have been cool. I knew she was joking about the "lost" part. But still, I kind of wished she'd agreed to come with me—even if she was a girl.

CHAPTER 4

The tunnels under the building were nothing like I expected. For one thing, they were heated. Ducts in the ceiling blew gusts of warm air on me as I walked by. For another thing they were well lit—not dark or damp. Finally, they were carpeted. What kind of tunnel is carpeted? If I hadn't taken the elevator down myself, I'd have guessed I was walking through an office building or a hotel.

I imagined the girl upstairs laughing her head off at my expense. I hadn't gotten her name, but I'd definitely have something to say to her when I went back out. *Don't get lost. Pay close attention to the signs.* There weren't any signs. And for a very good reason. There was only one tunnel—a long hallway that occasionally turned left or right, but never branched off. I couldn't have gotten lost if I'd wanted to.

The passageway was wide—at least eight feet across—and ten feet high. I imagined this was probably how they brought things like the handcart in and out of the store; that certainly would not have fit through the alley.

Eventually I reached an open door. Like the tunnel, the room was well lit. It looked a little like a library—filled with shelves of old books. Was this part of the business upstairs? It didn't look anything like the disorganized warehouse. Just inside the door was a long counter with the kind of silver bell that you ring by a pushing a button on the top. A three-by-five card taped to the counter read, "Ring for service." There didn't seem to be anyone in sight, so I pushed the bell.

Ping. A single chime echoed through the quiet room. As the noise died away, I realized another reason why the room reminded me of a library. It was quiet. Completely quiet. I listened for the sound of footsteps or rustling pages, but except for my own breathing, I couldn't hear a thing.

I leaned across the counter "Hello? Anybody home?" My voice sounded too loud in the silence that surrounded it. Although I couldn't see anyone, I wasn't about to go behind the counter. I'd learned my lesson upstairs. The last time, I'd only been surprised by a girl in a pioneer dress. But who knew what lived in the tunnels under the city? This time it could be a maniacal killer wielding a letter opener.

I wiped my palms on the front of my jeans and rang the bell again—louder this time. "Hey! Mr. Ladan," I called toward the stacks. "Are you back there?"

At the sound of my words, something shuffled around. The shuffling sound was followed by a yelp and then a huge crash— like someone had knocked over an entire shelf of books.

"Are you okay?" I yelled, wondering if I should go see what had happened.

"Fine! I'm fine!" a voice called back. "Just clearing some space." It was an old voice—kind of creaky and dry, like it hadn't been used a lot—but friendly. It didn't sound like the voice of a letter opener-wielding killer.

The sound of footsteps grew closer. "Who's there?" the voice called, although its owner was still hidden by the shelves.

"Kaleo Steele," I said, feeling a little weird talking to a bunch of books. "Brother Mortensen sent me."

"Of course. Of course." The voice sounded like it was just a few feet away, and, sure enough, a man arrived a second later. Several things about his appearance surprised me. The first was that he couldn't have been more than an inch or two over five feet—about the height of my nine-year-old brother. But his shoulders were nearly as broad as Crush's. Long gray hair, tied into a ponytail with a piece of cord, hung nearly to the middle of his back. I expected his skin to be pale from working in an underground library, but instead it was deeply tanned and leathery.

What surprised me most, though, was the way he held his hands out in front of him until they touched the counter. His fingers swept across the flat surface, found mine, and slid over my wrists and up my arms to my shoulders. His milky white eyes stared blankly at my face. He was blind.

"Perfect!" He grinned, revealing a set of big, white teeth. His hands patted my shoulders and reached to the top of my head. He was so short he had to stand on tiptoe to do it. "A tad bit too tall. But the right weight. Yes, you'll do wonderfully."

It was more than a little creepy having this odd, troll-like man patting me with fingers that felt as hard as wood. I tried to step back, but he held my arms in a surprisingly strong grip.

"Yes. You're the one all right. The one." He released me, and I quickly stepped away before he could grab me again.

I started to hold out the business card before it occurred to me he couldn't see it. "I'm, um, supposed to come see you," I said.

He didn't seem to be paying any attention. Instead he ducked below the counter and disappeared from view. From the moment I'd left practice, nothing had gone the way I'd expected it to. I didn't know why my meeting with Ladan should be any different. Still, this was weirder than weird.

I leaned over the counter, but all I could see was his back. He seemed to be rummaging around for something. "Brother Mortensen asked me to—" I started. But at that moment, Ladan sprang back up like a jack-in-the-box and slapped a shirt and a pair of pants on the counter. A second later he pulled out a jacket.

"What size shoe do you wear?" He stared at me with his empty eyes.

"I think you must have me confused with somebody else," I said, wondering if he wasn't a little crazy.

"I'm guessing eleven." He started coming around the counter. "But I'll find out soon enough."

The thought of him reaching out for my feet freaked me out. "Twelve," I blurted, backing away.

He snapped his fingers. "You're in luck!" He dashed away into the rows of shelves again.

I looked at the pile of clothes on the counter. Like the stuff upstairs, it seemed old. The shirt was made of some rough kind of fabric, and the buttons on the coat were made of metal—like little coins. But unlike most of the antique clothing I'd seen in museums, it didn't look faded or worn out. The pants were folded and pressed as if they were brand-new.

"Here you are," the man said, hurrying back into sight. He dropped a pair of clunky black boots onto the counter. "These should fit you perfectly."

"Look," I said as he shoved the piles of clothes toward me. "I don't know who you think I am, but I'm just here because Brother Mortensen made me promise I'd talk to you." I forced down the knot in my throat, knowing I'd have to tell this old man everything. "I . . . I went to a party with some kids at school. I didn't really want to but, well, I guess that doesn't matter. What matters is that I took a beer from this girl, and my seminary teacher saw me. If I don't get a note saying I met with you, I won't be able to play in the regional football game tomorrow."

I waited for the man to tell me what an idiot I'd been, or why a football game wasn't as important as my eternal salvation, or to quote scriptures. Whatever he had to say, I was ready for it. Instead he stood looking silently at me with those silvery eyes that couldn't see, but still seemed to be studying me.

I bit my lip. "Okay, I'll admit I really haven't been all that into the Church for the last couple of years."

He stared, his walnut-brown hands resting flat on the counter.

Apparently he wasn't letting me off the hook that easily. "I haven't prayed in I don't know how long. And I haven't been reading the scriptures." I chewed on the tip of my thumbnail, wishing he'd say something. "Look, I just don't buy into the whole Book of Mormon thing. Okay? I know it's a good story and all that. But that's all it is—a story. Maybe it helps some people, but I can't get excited about something that isn't real. I haven't told anyone this. Not even my parents. I . . . I don't have a testimony."

I'd never talked this way to anyone before, but here I was spilling my guts to a possibly crazy old man I'd met just a couple of minutes earlier. He raised a hand to his chin and rubbed it solemnly. Even though I knew his eyes couldn't see, I felt as if they were drilling right through me. I waited to hear him say something wise and meaningful.

He held out a single crooked finger and pointed to his left. "You can change in the storage room through that door."

□   □   □

"What am I doing here?" My words echoed off the low concrete ceiling as I walked in the direction the old man had pointed. The door he'd sent me through led to another tunnel.

Unlike the one I'd taken from the elevator, this one was dusty, and the ceiling was covered with pipes and cobwebs. It was also cold. I should have been home eating dinner and resting for the game. Instead, I was watching my own breath float up from my lips and playing dress-up with some blind guy.

And what was all that about anyway? What was with the clothes, and why was a guy who couldn't see working with a room full of books? None of it made sense, and all of it ticked me off. About thirty feet down the hall, I came to an intersection.

What am I supposed to do now? I thought, clutching the clothes in my arms. I looked down each of the dimly lit tunnels, but none of them had a door I could see. I turned back the way I'd come and considered asking for directions. I'd probably get another blank stare for my trouble.

The hallway to the left smelled like something had died in it, and the one straight ahead was empty for at least another fifty feet. That left the one on the right. Of course I hadn't walked more than a minute before I came to a dead end. Just my luck.

I gritted my teeth and returned to the intersection. Figuring I was going to end up there anyway, I tried the hall that smelled like dirty feet and rotten vegetables. Sure enough, I passed a stack of crates and found a partly open door. Of course the stench was coming from whatever was inside the room. Moldy cardboard boxes and a metal barrel with a green layer of fuzz on top of it looked like they hadn't been touched in years.

"Stupid!" I grunted, kicking off my sneakers and dropping the clothes onto a folding metal chair. I started to toss my sweatshirt onto the floor but decided to hang it on the top of the door instead. Who knew what that green fuzz was?

The more I thought about it, the more I suspected my seminary teacher was playing some kind of trick on me. Undoubtedly the old guy was in on it as well. As I yanked off my jeans, I could just imagine Brother Mortensen laughing and wondering how long it would take me to figure out they'd been pulling my leg. Well, the joke was over. Really funny. I was getting my note and getting out of this place.

Lacing up the boots, I realized someone had pulled off the labels. There were no markings of any kind—not even a note to show the size. And I could see actual nails buried in the sole. The coat was warm enough, but like the rest of the clothes, it didn't have any labels either. Not that it mattered. I was only wearing this lame outfit long enough to get my note.

As I stepped out into the frigid hallway, I suddenly had the feeling someone was watching me. I spun around, expecting to see eyes peering from the dim length of the hall. I even glanced back into the room, although no one could have entered it without me seeing. The hallway and the room were both empty. But I still couldn't shake the feeling someone was nearby. Goose bumps rose on the backs of my arms. This whole thing was way too creepy. Something made a sound—the same kind of skittering noise I'd heard outside the alley. Without looking back, I ran.

I've never really enjoyed books where people end up some place they didn't expect—Alice in Wonderland falling into a tree, the kid who rolls away in a giant piece of fruit, Harry Potter going to a magic school. I know where I'm going and why. I don't want anyone messing with my plans.

CHAPTER 5

I put on the clothes!" I said, slamming open the door to the
book room. "Now I want—"

I stopped and looked around, my pulse pounding as
much from fear as from anger. The old guy wasn't even there.
"Hey," I shouted. "Ladan—if that's your real name—the joke's
over. I have to get home before my mom grounds me for life."

There was no answer.

"Where are you?" I leaned across the counter, but I couldn't
see him. "Probably deaf as well as blind," I muttered.

I looked at the low swinging door that separated the front
of the counter from the back. But I didn't want to go through it
now any more than I had the first time. The room felt empty,
but it also felt—I don't know, watchful or something—like the
books had eyes. It was stupid. I knew that. The guys would rag
on me for the rest of the year if they could see me. But that
didn't change how I felt.

I started to check my watch before realizing I'd left it in

the storage room. It had to be nearly 7:30. Even if I left right now, I still might not make it home by eight.

"Come on!" I yelled. "What did you do? Forget about me and leave?"

The thought that the old man had done just that—left before I could get my note—got me moving. I swung open the door and stepped behind the counter. No alarms went off. No lights flashed.

"Excuse me?" I found myself talking quietly again, as if I was in a library. Which I guess I was. Moving around to look straight down the stacks of books, I could see the room was much bigger than it looked at first. Bigger than I ever could have imagined. The shelves seemed to go on for miles. The old guy could be anywhere. Or he could be nowhere. I could be in this big empty room full of books all by myself. What if the elevator didn't work after closing? Or what if I got halfway down the aisle and the lights suddenly went out?

I turned around—I'd leave without the note—and found myself standing only inches away from a gray, wrinkled face looking up at me.

"Ha laa!" I gasped, stumbling backward. It was a Hawaiian phrase my mother used when something surprised her. Usually I didn't speak much Hawaiian, but the old guy, who had somehow slipped right behind me without a sound, shocked it out me.

"Aloha ahiahi," he calmly said, as though he hadn't just scared me silly.

"*Good evening!* Good evening?" I gulped, trying to catch

my breath. It didn't occur to me at the time that he'd spoken Hawaiian too. Or that he'd managed to stop just a few inches away from me, even though he couldn't see. "What is it with you and that girl upstairs? Are you both trying to scare me to death?"

If my anger upset him, he didn't show it. Instead he ran a gnarled hand over my shoulder and down my arm, and nodded. "Does it itch?"

"What?"

"The shirt," he said, patting my chest. "Does it itch?"

"No." I stepped away from him and his silver eyes. "A little, maybe. What does it matter?"

"It's wool. I wove it myself. Would you like to see the loom?" He stepped toward me, and I backed away.

"No. I just want my note."

"I made it to fit *him*," he said, still coming toward me. "You know, you're nearly his size. A few inches taller, like his brother. But you both have the same broad shoulders."

He was crazy. There was no question about it. But maybe if I played along for a few minutes I could get the note and still be home by eight-thirty. "Who? Who am I the same size as?"

"Joseph Smith, of course."

Suddenly it all came together. This guy wasn't crazy. And neither was Brother Mortensen. At least not psycho-ward crazy. "That's what this is all about. You wanted me to dress up like Joseph Smith so I would feel guilty about not believing in the Book of Mormon. It's one of those—what do you call them—object lessons."

"Object lesson?" Ladan tried to look surprised, but I had it figured out now.

"Nice try. But it won't work. I've already been down this road before. I did the whole handcart experience. Yes, it made me feel sorry for the pioneers. It even made me appreciate what they suffered for their religion. But that doesn't change the fact that they did it all for nothing. I'm sure Joseph Smith was a good man, but that doesn't make the Book of Mormon true."

I pushed open the swinging door to the other side of the counter, expecting the old man to let me have it now that I was onto his trick. Instead he tugged at the end of his long gray ponytail and grinned. "He was a criminal, you know."

"What? Who was a criminal?" For a minute I thought he was talking about me.

"Joseph Smith. You called him a good man, but he was a criminal. He was arrested many, many times. He was even killed in jail."

Ladan was playing games again. Every Latter-day Saint kid knew about Joseph Smith being arrested, you learned that stuff clear back in Primary. "They threw him in jail because they didn't like what he taught. He wasn't guilty of any crimes. But that doesn't make him a real prophet."

"Prophet!" Ladan spat on the ground. His look of disgust was so real, I'd almost have believed it if I didn't know he was messing with me. "He was a liar and a cheat."

He wanted me to defend Joseph Smith so he could trick me into admitting he was really a prophet. But I wasn't buying it. "I'm not saying *everything* he said was a lie. I'm just saying the Book of Mormon didn't come from some ancient gold record. Who knows? Maybe he dreamed about the angel and made the rest up. He was just a kid. I don't blame him as much as I blame the people who believed him."

Ladan's silver eyes seemed to blaze. I thought he was upset that I'd figured out his plan, but what he said next shocked even me. "Do you realize how many deaths that man is responsible for?"

I shook my head. I'd never actually considered the idea.

"Hundreds!" he shouted, his mouth pulled down into a grimace. "People were shot, tortured, left their families, lost their homes, their jobs, their money, their lives—all because they believed in a piece of fiction sold by a charlatan as the word of God. How can you call a man who would allow that to happen anything but wicked?"

I shook my head, feeling sick inside. I guessed that when I'd thought about it at all, I'd lumped Joseph Smith in with all the other religious fanatics: ministers, priests, the Holy Rollers who preached on TV and the radio. Just another guy who was convinced he knew what God wanted. Not bad, just confused.

"Your name means *voice*," Ladan said. I looked up, surprised. "If you knew a story you had made up or even stolen was false, wouldn't you speak out when you realized how many people were leaving their homes and families because of it? *Dying* because of it?"

I swallowed. "I guess."

"You *guess?*" he thundered, his voice echoing off the ceiling. "Have you read that book?"

"Not all of it," I admitted.

He nodded, his chin pointing out at me like the prow of a ship. "Do you believe such nonsense as golden balls that only work if you are obedient? Rocks that light up? Sailing across the ocean in ships that look like a pair of wooden bowls glued together?"

I shook my head.

"Of course you don't. Who could believe things like three men living until the return of Christ? *Nephites!*" He grinned—his blind eyes twinkling—and for a moment I thought he was laughing at my expense. Then I realized he was making fun of the idea of the Three Nephites.

I was confused. "If you don't believe in it either, why are you here? Why did Brother Mortensen send me to see you?"

Ladan's face crinkled as he leaned toward me. "He sent you here to learn the truth."

That wasn't at all what I'd expected to hear. And I wished I'd never come. As long as I thought of Joseph Smith as a good man with an overactive imagination, I could at least pretend to be Mormon. But how could I keep going to church knowing what I knew? How could I let my friends spend two years of their lives teaching lies?

"Have I taught you?" The old man reached over the counter and grabbed the lapels of my jacket. He was so close I could feel his warm breath on my face. I could see a tiny bubble of spit in the corner of his mouth.

My throat felt so dry I could barely speak. I was wearing clothes designed for a wicked man. A liar. Maybe even a murderer. They suddenly felt far too tight. "Yes."

As he straightened, I could hear his spine crack. "Good," he said, putting a hand to his back. "Then you may change back into your own clothes and leave."

I started toward the door before remembering why I'd come in the first place. "What about my note?"

He poked the tip of his tongue out from his lips and tilted his head. "I've written everything you need. It will be here for you once you've changed."

□   □   □

Walking back down the hallway, I felt like I'd swallowed an icicle. My stomach was numb, and my throat was raw. What had just happened? Had Brother Mortensen really wanted me to learn that Joseph Smith was a horrible person? That didn't feel right. Did he think Ladan was someone else? That his message would be different? That seemed more likely. But how could he make such a mistake?

I thought back over the points the old man had used. His logic seemed sound enough. I could no longer tell myself the Book of Mormon was a simple fantasy novel like I had in the past. It had cost too much in lives and sacrifice. Anyone who would let people die over a lie was not a person to be looked up to.

So was Joseph Smith an evil man?

It went against everything I'd been taught. Everything I'd

felt. But I'd only heard the story from one side. I'd never made any sacrifices for the Church. I didn't know anyone who'd given their life for the gospel. I thought about the girl I'd met upstairs with the props. She seemed to believe in the Church. She'd said her great-great-something grandmother was one of the first converts. Maybe that was why she had looked at me so oddly when I showed her Ladan's card. Maybe she knew what he would say.

The tunnel felt colder than I remembered it, and a low mist clung to the floor, like in one of those old black-and-white horror movies they show late at night. All the more reason to get out of here and get home. Next thing you know, I'd stumble into a nest of rats.

There was one thing that didn't make sense though. If Joseph Smith had let all those people believe a lie—had encouraged them to believe it—he *had* to be an evil person. But why would an evil man write a book encouraging people to do good things? I was the first to admit I hadn't read the Book of Mormon cover to cover. But what I'd read seemed to teach some pretty good concepts. Be kind to others. Honor your parents. Live a Christlike life. Why would a person who was so bad write a book telling people to be good?

Money? I was no historian, but from what I could remember, I didn't think Joseph Smith was ever rich. In fact, it seemed like he was usually living in other people's homes. That didn't sound like he was rolling in cash.

Power? Maybe. People followed him and did what he said.

At least sometimes. But what did that get him? I couldn't remember him using his office to gain special benefits.

Fame? I paused in the middle of the cold, dark hallway. Could that be it? Some authors got really famous for their books. The author who wrote the Harry Potter books was famous. So were Mark Twain and Shakespeare. Maybe Joseph Smith wrote the Book of Mormon to be famous. There still seemed to be something wrong with that logic, but I was too tired to worry about it.

Looking around, I realized I must have passed the hall that led me to the nasty room where I'd left my clothes. The tunnel I was in now looked narrower and a little shorter than the one I remembered. That's what I got for thinking about religion when I needed to be worrying about tomorrow's football game.

I pulled my hands up into the sleeves of my jacket to keep them warm and jogged back to the crossing hallway. It didn't seem to smell as bad this time. Or maybe I was just used to it. Either way, I was in a hurry to change clothes and get home. But when I passed the pile of boxes and went to open the door, I found a blank wall. Well, not completely blank. Bolted to the concrete was a metal sign that looked like something you might see on the side of the road. Instead of a speed limit, or a warning to watch for ice though, were the words, "Seek, and ye shall find."

I stopped and turned around slowly. Was this some kind of joke? I ran my hands across the smooth wall. I was sure this was where I'd entered the storage room, but while Ladan was capable of a lot, I couldn't see him making a door disappear.

Obviously I'd gone down the wrong hallway. I must have walked farther than I thought while I was thinking about Joseph Smith. As soon as I realized my mistake, I was able to laugh at myself for freaking out a little. Weird thing with the sign, though.

Not that it mattered. I didn't care about signs, or hallways. I cared about getting out of the tunnels. I walked down the hallway again, this time paying attention to where I was going. When I reached the first corner, I turned right. Straight ahead would be Ladan's office. To the right would be the stinky hallway.

But when I reached the next intersection, there was no right, only a dark passage leading to the left. It was cobwebby, and most of the lights were out. It looked clogged with a bunch of junk. And there was another one of those weird signs. This one had an arrow pointing toward the cobwebs, and beneath the arrow were the words, "We are such stuff as dreams are made on."

"Shakespeare," I whispered, rubbing my hands across my arms to stay warm. It was a quote from the *Tempest,* a play we'd been studying in English. I'd just been thinking about Shakespeare. It was simply a weird coincidence, but I didn't remember seeing any signs the first time I walked through these hallways.

For a quick second, I had the disturbing thought that somehow I'd entered an entirely different set of hallways. Except that was impossible. I'd left the book room through the same door as before, and while I might have been distracted,

I knew I wouldn't have turned down another tunnel without noticing.

I'd simply gone farther than I thought. The reason I hadn't seen the signs was because I hadn't gone straight through the intersection the first time. Feeling reassured, I continued to walk down the hallway. My stomach growled, and I thought about dinner. The feast wouldn't be until tomorrow, but I might be able to sneak a piece of roast pork tonight. And some of the really good coconut-pineapple bread my mom made.

It took me longer than I thought it should have to reach the next intersection, and when I did, I knew at once something was wrong. For one thing, there was no bad smell. For another, the lights were single bulbs hanging from wires, not the fluorescents that had been there before. And there was another sign: "All that glitters is not gold."

My heart took a crazy thump. I turned around slowly, trying to regain my sense of direction. The book room was straight ahead. Or was it? It should have been. But part of me felt sure it was off to the right.

Pay close attention to the signs. You don't want to get lost down there. The voice of the girl upstairs echoed in my ears. The fog that was ankle-high before now came up to my knees—swirling in freaky twists and turns, even though there was no breeze that I could feel.

"Calm down," I said, my voice bouncing off the ceiling that seemed lower than I remembered. There couldn't be that many tunnels under a city the size of Salt Lake, and I hadn't walked more than five minutes. Ten, at the most. As I walked back the way I'd come, I started reviewing football plays to keep myself from losing it. "Double Tight, power eye formation 32. Pro-Set, slot left. Eagle-eye pro-set formation, twins right, slot z right."

My words dried up as I reached the hallway I'd paused at only a minute before. The tunnel was still cobwebby and dark, but now it seemed to veer off to one side instead of going straight out at a ninety-degree angle. I looked up at the sign, and for a moment couldn't pull air into my lungs.

The sign that had been a Shakespeare quote only a few minutes before now read, "A fool and his money are soon parted."

"This can't be right," I said, my voice trembling. I wiped my palm across my forehead, and it came away damp and cold. Getting turned around while I wasn't paying attention was one thing. But this time, I'd been watching exactly where I was going. This *was* the corner I'd stopped at before. I hadn't made a mistake. And yet it clearly wasn't the same corner. For the first time, I could feel real panic taking hold. When I was a kid, my dad always told me that if you got lost in the woods, you should avoid panic at all costs. "Sit still and hug a tree," he said. "Someone will find you if you stay in one place. It's the people who lose their heads—who start running instead of staying where they are—that stay lost."

But there were no trees down here. And who would come looking for me, even if I stayed where I was? My parents had no idea where I'd gone, and who knew if Ladan would even remember me by the next morning? Thinking of my parents suddenly made me remember my cell phone. If I had service down here, I could call for help. I could explain to my mom what—

I reached for my pocket, but instead of finding the denim of my old jeans, my fingers touched a rough, unfamiliar fabric. I couldn't bear to look down, and I didn't need to see to know that my cell phone was back with my wallet in my pants pocket.

I couldn't even pretend I wasn't scared now. In my mind, I knew I couldn't be more than a few hundred yards from getting out. It didn't make any sense to have tunnels that didn't lead to somewhere. But there was something wrong with these tunnels. Something that made me think of abandoned mines, and a maze with a minotaur in the center.

"Don't freak out. Don't freak out," I repeated to myself as I began jogging up one tunnel and down another. But the longer I went without seeing a door, the less I could hold back my fear. New tunnels branched off right and left. Some of them were flat, but more and more of them sloped up or down. The fog was almost up to my chest now, dancing and spinning like something was racing through it just out of my sight. It didn't feel like I was only thirty or forty feet under the city anymore. It felt like hundreds—like being deep in the Timpanogos caves.

Signs flashed by like crazy warnings. Some of them I recognized, but others made no sense at all: "Don't take any wooden nickels." "A stitch in time saves nine." "Keep your powder dry." "Remember the Alamo." "Some things are better left unsaid." "Dead men tell no tales."

Suddenly I skidded to a halt. The concrete under my feet was damp and slippery, and I nearly fell. But I wasn't paying attention to the ground. I was looking up. What I saw there made my tongue stick to the roof of my mouth. When I'd first entered the tunnels, they'd been lit by fluorescent lights. A few minutes ago I'd noticed that the fluorescents had been replaced by single bulbs hanging from frayed cords. But the light above my head wasn't a bulb at all. It was a flickering yellow flame dancing at the end of a hissing gas jet.

I looked at the sign below the gas lamp, and a moan forced itself from my throat. This had to be some kind of really weird, twisted dream. If only I could make myself wake up. But it didn't feel like a dream; it felt like a nightmare. The sign read, "Crush says hi."

Unable to hold back the panic any longer, I raced from one hall to another. I didn't look at the signs or the lights. I didn't care about them. I only wanted to find one thing. As I turned a downward-sloping corner, the soles of my boots skidded on the wet floor, and I hit the ground hard.

Lying on the icy concrete, I didn't care that I had gotten into this mess by taking a beer, or that I wasn't sure anyone was listening. I pressed my eyes closed as tightly as I could, and begged God to help me. "Please, Heavenly Father, let me find a way out of this. Help me out of this maze, and I promise I'll start going to seminary again. I swear I'll never take another beer."

After finishing my prayer, I opened my eyes. I was sitting on the floor of a dark hall with walls that seemed to be made of crumbling rock. Fifty feet ahead, the tunnel ended in a blank wall. Another dead end. I started to turn around before realizing something was different about the wall at the end.

It was made of dark wooden planks instead of stone. Strange symbols were scratched into the wood. I stared at them, and for a minute, they seemed to blur and change into letters before my eyes. *K-n-something-something-l-e-d-something-something F-a* . . . But I didn't care about the words. What was below them on the left almost made me cry with relief. A silver doorknob.

I was sure it would be locked, that this would be another trick. But when I ran to the door and grabbed the knob, it twisted in my hands. I pushed the door open and plunged through. Fresh air washed over me as I stumbled out into a grassy field. The sky opening above my head was the most wonderful sight I'd ever seen.

I was so happy to be free of the tunnels that it took me a moment to realize I could see trees and grass and dirt. I looked up at a sky washed with purple and orange. The snow had stopped falling, and the air felt far less cold than when I'd arrived. The sun was coming up. It was morning.

I'd been trapped in the tunnels all night.

I was either going crazy, or this was the most elaborate object lesson ever. It totally blew away the one with the food coloring and the bleach.

CHAPTER 6

At first all I could do was stand bent over with my hands on my knees, waiting for my heart to stop pounding and trying to catch my breath. Could I really have been running blindly all night? I'd been afraid before, but never so badly that I lost track of time.

Little by little, my pulse evened out, and I began to notice my surroundings. After escaping those bizarre tunnels, the everyday normalness of trees and grass should have calmed me down, but what I saw only made me more uneasy.

I guessed I could accept that I'd been lost all night, even though it felt like only an hour or two had passed at most. The sun was up, so I really didn't have any choice. And since the sun *was* up, it made sense that it should be warmer. But it felt like the temperature was in the high-forties or low-fifties, which it hadn't been for weeks. Still, those were changes I could accept if I had to. Other things were not so easy.

For one thing, I'd parked my car in the middle of

downtown Salt Lake. No matter how lost I got, I couldn't imagine the underground tunnels leading out of the city. And I knew I hadn't run more than a couple of miles. Now I was standing in a clearing of what looked like fairly thick woods. Maybe I'd come out in a park of some kind. But what park anywhere near downtown was so deep that I couldn't see any signs of buildings or roads?

That was another thing. It was late November. All the leaves had been off the trees for at least a month. But the trees around me were still covered with bright reds, oranges, and yellows. I wasn't a plant specialist by a long shot, but I'd been camping plenty of times. And a few of the trees around me didn't look like anything I'd ever seen on my camping trips.

Then there was the weirdest thing of all. When I left practice, the snow was almost six inches deep along the sidelines of the football field—more in the shady spots. Looking around now, I couldn't see so much as a patch of white. Something was seriously out of whack here.

I turned slowly in place. It seemed like I could hear the buzz of every insect in the tall grass. The tat-tat-tat of what I guessed was a woodpecker was crystal clear in the morning air. And a squirrel, or whatever it was bouncing around the branches over my head, sounded right on top of me. There was definitely nothing wrong with my hearing, but no matter how hard I tried, I couldn't hear the sound of a car, a voice, or even a dog barking.

The hair on my arms and neck prickled like I'd just been zapped with a charge of static electricity.

Where the heck was I? And how did I get here? Was this part of what Brother Mortensen wanted me to learn? If this was some kind of an object lesson, it was the most amazing one ever.

"I don't have time for this," I said, shaking my head to break out of whatever spell had been holding me in place. This was a good trick. Somehow Ladan and my seminary teacher had managed to get me lost and led me here—wherever here was. The sun was just above the horizon, which made it about eight. Which meant I had a game in just over two hours! My coach would have a fit if I was late. And my—

Suddenly I remembered my parents. They'd be totally going nuts. They probably called the police when I didn't come home last night. I had to get to a phone or missing a football game would be the least of my worries.

Panic filled me all over again as I pictured my mother's face when I told her I'd spent the night in a maze of tunnels under the city. Somehow I didn't think she'd believe me when I told her it was all my seminary teacher's fault.

There was no obvious path, so I started running toward a break in the trees. I'd barely reached the edge of the woods when my clunky boots caught on a root, and I fell flat on my face. My right hand scraped against the edge of a sharp rock, and the air whooshed out of my lungs.

"Very smooth," I said when I could breathe again. "The All-American wide receiver in action." I looked at my hand. There was a pretty deep cut, and blood was smeared across the palm, but I didn't think I would need stitches. I wiped the blood off on the leg of my pants, not caring whether Ladan had made them himself or not.

I started to stand up and noticed something lying on the grass in front of me. It looked like an envelope. It must have fallen out of my jacket when I tripped. I picked it up. The paper was brownish and kind of brittle, like it was old, but my name was printed across the front in a shaky handwriting.

A message from Ladan? I remembered him grabbing my lapels just before he sent me to change clothes. The back of the envelope was sealed with a blob of red wax. Stamped into the wax were three interlocking Ns.

Still sitting on the ground, I ripped open the brown paper. Something fell out. It took me a minute of digging through the grass to find it, but finally I pulled out a small black rod with a kind of clover-shaped handle on one end. The rod was no longer than my pinky, and made out of some kind of metal. It had a series of shallow grooves carved into it. Even though I knew I had to get moving, I sat for a second turning the metal rod in my hands and trying to figure out what it was. It looked like one of those old-fashioned keys, but missing the actual part that turned the lock.

I checked the envelope and pulled out a single piece of paper. It was not quite as brown as the envelope, but it also felt old. The front of the page was covered with words written in the same spiky writing as my name. I read the first paragraph.

"And the key of the house of David will I lay upon his shoulder; so he shall open, and none shall shut; and he shall shut, and none shall open."

It sounded like some kind of scripture. But what did it mean?

The second paragraph was written directly to me.

Kaleo,

I hope the tunnels weren't too frightening. They are a lot like life. If you don't pay attention to where you're going—and sometimes even if you do—you can find yourself lost and confused. The signs of man may lead you astray, but the word of God never will. Knowledge is the key, and faith the power to turn it. Together they will allow you to open the door and return.

It was signed at the bottom with,

Good luck,
From one witness to another,
Jadan

What was that supposed to mean?

I flipped the paper over and saw what looked like a map

on the back, complete with a compass labeled East, West, North, and South. Toward the bottom of the map was a picture of a door. *The one I'd come through?* On the right side was a straight line with Canandaigua Road written along the side. Closer to the top was another road labeled Armington. I'd never heard of Canandaigua or Armington, but if I could find either of them, I could get to a phone and call my parents.

Near the bottom of the map was what looked like a fence of some kind. An arrow pointed to a tall tree surrounded by three rocks in a triangle shape. Written beneath it was, "Begin your journey of faith here. But hurry. It will be dark soon."

I turned the paper over and read Ladan's message again. It sounded like a lesson. Obviously the metal rod was supposed to be a key. I looked over my shoulder at the door I'd come through. It was set in the side of a grassy hill as if it had been built into it.

If Ladan thought I was going back in there, he was crazy. And I definitely wasn't going on any crazy scavenger hunt. They could keep their faith and knowledge, I was going home. Their stupid game was over. I nearly tossed the key back into the grass. Instead, I shoved it into the envelope along with the letter. Here was evidence I could show my mom that this wasn't my fault.

At least the letter proved one thing. Ladan was tricky, but he wasn't perfect. The letter said I had to hurry before it got dark. He must have thought it would take me longer to find my way out than it had. It was barely morning.

I looked up at the sun, and my fingers slowly crunched the

letter. I tried to swallow, but my throat wouldn't work. This was impossible. Totally, completely, impossible. I might have run all night. I could have lost ten or twelve hours in my panic. But definitely no more than that.

And yet the sun that had been just above the horizon a few minutes ago was now beginning to edge below it. The bottom was already hidden. It wasn't early morning like I'd thought. It was evening. Saturday evening. Somehow I'd been gone almost twenty-four hours—an entire day. I'd already missed the game.

□   □   □

I couldn't believe it. How could a whole day have passed? If I'd actually eaten or drunk anything, I might have thought Ladan had drugged me. But I hadn't eaten anything since lunch. That made me realize something else. If my last meal was more than twenty-four hours ago, I should be starving. I *was* hungry, but I didn't feel like I'd gone twenty-four hours without eating.

Looking at the sun—which I could practically see dropping behind the horizon as I watched—and feeling a breeze which was far too warm for late-November, I began to understand things were much more wrong than I'd realized. Whatever was going on was so totally messed up, I didn't want any part of it. Suddenly the tunnels didn't seem that bad after all. At least I knew they were under the streets of Salt Lake.

The sky was turning from blue to orange as I walked across the clearing to the door. Soon it would be night. This place felt wrong in so many ways. I didn't know where I was, but I knew

I didn't want to be here. And I definitely didn't want to be here when it was night.

I tried to open the door, but the knob that had turned so easily before refused to budge. I jiggled and yanked at it. I pushed the door and pulled. The wood looked old, and maybe even a little rotten. But when I tried to kick it down, pain jolted up my leg like I'd tried to kick down a steel wall. Then I saw the keyhole. It had a circle at the top and a triangle part at the bottom. The sort of old-fashioned keyhole people peek through in old movies.

Quickly I shook the little black rod out of the envelope. I shoved it into the hole. It fit. When I turned it, though, it spun around and around. There was no click. The knob still wouldn't budge. I pulled out the letter and reread the message.

Knowledge is the key, and faith the power to turn it. Together they will allow you to open the door and return.

What did that mean? If this little black rod wasn't the key, what was I supposed to with it?

It was starting to get dark. I flipped over the sheet.

Begin your journey of faith here.

Ladan wanted me to head out into the woods at night. Whatever the moral of this lesson was, I wanted no part of it.

I slammed my fist against the door. The thump was dull and muted, like I'd slammed my hand into the side of a mountain. In my mind I pictured, not a tunnel behind the wooden planks, but a solid mound of dirt and rock. I thought I'd escaped when I found my way out of the tunnel. But I hadn't. I'd just moved from one trap into another.

"No!" I screamed, pounding and kicking at the door. "Let me in. Ladan! Brother Mortensen! This isn't funny. I don't care about the football game. I just want to go home."

I wonder how Superman felt when he discovered he could fly, run faster than a train, and check whether his car needed an oil change without lifting the hood. Was he like, "Wow, this is the coolest thing ever"? Or did he maybe think, "This is just a little too weird for me. I'm going back home on the next rocket"?

CHAPTER 7

The sun was completely down by the time I began making my way through the woods, and the moon hadn't yet come up. Surprisingly, I found that I could actually see quite well, even in the dark. That didn't make me any less nervous. If the woods had seemed quiet before, now they felt absolutely dead—except when a twig or branch would crack off in the distance, and I'd spin around, sure someone was sneaking up on me.

This afternoon—or yesterday afternoon, whichever it was—seemed like weeks before. I replayed the scenes over and over in my head as I pushed my way through thick underbrush and branches that scratched at my hands and face. In my imaginary conversation, I never gave Crush the chance to invite me to his behind-the-bleachers party. "Dude, I'm going straight home," I said, before he could get a word out of his mouth. "Now get out of my face."

I didn't realize I'd spoken out loud until something burst

66

out of the trees to my right. At first I thought it was a small, red dog. But it didn't bark or growl. Instead it stood frozen in place, staring at me. As I watched it watching me, I realized it wasn't a dog at all. Its ears were too long and pointed. Its fur was red, but its muzzle and the front of its chest were white, and its long slender legs were black.

It stared at me a moment longer, gave a high-pitched yip, as if scolding me for invading its space, then raced back into the woods. "A fox," I whispered under my breath. Except for at the zoo, I'd never seen a wild animal so close before. And I'd seen the fox so clearly.

I glanced up, thinking the moon must have come out to provide so much light, and was surprised to see that the canopy of leaves above me blocked out the sky completely. I couldn't see a single star, and I definitely couldn't see the moon. So how could I have seen the fox so clearly? Another mystery that made no sense.

I tried to keep walking west, the direction of the road according to the map, but without the sun, it was hard to know if I was going the right way. I could only keep myself on a somewhat straight line by using a trick I'd learned in Scouts. I picked an object in the distance—a tree, a rock, or a bush— and walked to it. Then I picked another one and walked to that. The map hadn't shown any scale of distances, so I had no idea whether the road was a mile away or ten. Eventually I came across a narrow dirt path and began following that.

What I knew for sure was that I definitely wasn't in Salt Lake anymore. There are plenty of woods in Utah, but nothing so deep or quiet anywhere within walking distance of the city—at least not without heading up into the canyons. And the gently rolling hills I was walking up and down were not anywhere in the canyons. There had to be some kind of explanation for what was happening to me, but I sure couldn't think of one.

I didn't realize I'd reached the big tree until I saw the first of the three rocks. It was four or five feet tall and shaped a little like an arrowhead. The surface was grayish-white and sort of glittery. When I saw another rock fifteen or twenty feet away, I looked up at the tree between the two of them. It was a giant all right—just as the map said—towering above the rest of the trees like a basketball center looming over a bunch of puny point guards.

Sure enough, when I looked off to the right, I saw the third stone in the pattern. *Begin your journey of faith here,* the letter read. I looked around, wondering if someone was supposed to meet me.

"Anybody here?" I called, not sure if I hoped for an answer or not. On the one hand, I really wanted to talk to someone—to ask them where I was and what was going on. On the other hand, with all the weirdness that had happened already, I wouldn't have been surprised to run into an elf or a dwarf.

When no one responded to my shout, I walked to the tree and looked around. I thought maybe I'd find another envelope with more directions, but if it was there, I couldn't spot it. I kicked around the leaves and twigs, but all I managed to stir up was a little ratlike thing that squeaked and ran deeper into the woods.

"What now?" I asked. After all my walking, my legs ached and my back felt like I'd been nailed in the open field by a strong safety. I didn't know how long I'd actually gone without a meal, but my stomach was complaining up a storm. I figured I might as well continue on to the road. Whatever I was supposed to find didn't seem to be here, and the sooner I found a road, the sooner I could find a house—and a phone.

First though, I'd take a little break. These boots might have been handmade, but Air Jordans they were not. I could feel blisters on the backs of both of my heels. I dropped to the ground, leaned my head back against the side of the rock, and stretched out my legs with a sigh.

I closed my eyes and listened as a breeze rustled the leaves overhead. Now that the sun was gone, the air was starting to cool down. It wasn't nearly as cold as it had been the night I'd driven into the city, but I also wasn't wearing the down jacket I'd had on then. The coat I was wearing now was thick, but if I didn't find someplace to spend the night, I would be hurting by the morning.

I rubbed my hands together, trying to warm them up, and felt something strange. The skin on my right hand seemed . . . odd. Holding my palm out in front of my face, I shook my head. A lot of crazy things had happened today, but this was more than wrong. I got to my feet and stepped into the moonlight just to be sure of what I was seeing.

I ran the fingers of my left hand over the skin of my right, just in case my eyes were fooling me. The cut I'd gotten less than an hour before, when I fell on the rock, was gone. Not scabbed over. Not smaller. Completely gone. The blood was gone too. I turned my hand over and back. The skin looked new and smooth. The smoothness was what I'd felt before—like the skin of a baby.

For a second I wondered if I'd only imagined tripping over the root and cutting my hand on the rock. I felt for the letter in my pocket. It was there. And I could feel the key inside the envelope. I *had* fallen. Could I have imagined the cut? No. I'd definitely given my palm a good gash. I remembered wiping my hand on—

I glanced down at my pant leg and stumbled backward with a little, "Huh?" of surprise. Even the blood I'd wiped on my pants was gone.

"No way," I breathed, trying to keep from losing it again. Everything around me being messed up was one thing. Someone had changed the leaves, the weather, the snow, even the time. That was bad. But if a cut I knew I'd had an hour before was gone, that meant *I* was the one messed up. Not once had I considered that I might be losing my marbles, but now . . .

People didn't just magically heal from their cuts. There was no explanation whatsoever that could explain that. Which meant I hadn't cut myself in the first place. Which meant . . .

I wasn't sure what that meant. But I had to prove to myself my injuries didn't just go away. If I only had another . . .

I remembered my elbow—the one I'd scraped on the box of buttons. The girl with the props had put a bandage on it. As long as that was still there, I wasn't cracking up. I pulled off my coat and rolled up the sleeve of my shirt. The bandage was right where she'd put it. With a soft laugh of relief, I peeled back the bandage. This place might be totally screwed up but I was—

"No," I gasped, pulling off the bandage completely and staring. "No, no, no. This isn't right." The scrape was gone. The skin was pink and clean. There wasn't even a single drop of blood on the bandage.

I dropped to the ground and pulled off my boots and socks. I had blisters; I'd felt them when I sat down. People who healed themselves didn't have blisters. But when I looked at my heels, there were no marks, no bubbles. The skin wasn't red or raw. I ran my hands across my feet, and there was no pain. Stretching my legs, I realized my muscles were no longer sore either.

"Okay," I said, breathing in deep gasps. "There has to be an explanation for this. I have no stinking idea what the explanation is, but I'm sure there is one."

Since I'd arrived here I'd somehow developed the ability to heal my wounds without realizing it. And I could see in the dark. Even my hearing seemed better. What could have caused all of this?

"I got bitten by a radioactive spider?"

Nope. No tingling spider-sense.

"I got too close to an experimental gamma bomb?"

As far as I could tell, my skin wasn't turning green, and

even when I'd tried to knock the door down, I hadn't developed huge muscles or ripped out of my clothes.

"Could I have been sent to a different universe where I have superhuman powers?"

At first that seemed the most likely answer. It felt as if I were on another world. But what were the odds of another world having the same kinds of plants, animals, and atmosphere as Earth? Besides, even when I concentrated on it, I couldn't see through things or fly.

So apparently I wasn't a superhero. At least not any of the ones I knew. I tried to think of what someone would name a superhero who could see foxes in the dark, hear crickets, and heal blisters faster than a speeding bullet. Nothing especially inspiring came to mind, but at least the process helped calm me down.

It seemed that my super powers didn't extend to withstanding cold. My feet were freezing, and I was starting to shiver, so I pulled on my jacket and put my socks and boots back on my feet.

Although I was still freaked out, I wasn't *freaking* out. I considered the whole thing might be a dream—that I'd slipped on a patch of ice and gone into a coma or something—but as far as I could remember I'd never had a dream this detailed. And if I'd dreamed up super powers, I was sure I could have come up with something better than healing blisters and scrapes. At this point, all I could do was be grateful my blisters were gone and see what came next.

I didn't have long to wait. As I was tying my second boot, I heard voices.

"Over here," called a male voice.

"Get out of my way," snarled a second voice. "You nearly tripped me."

"I wouldn't 'a tripped you if you hadn't stepped right in front of me."

I was so happy to hear human voices, I nearly shouted out until a third voice hissed, "Shut up, both o' you. He might hear us."

If they were trying to be quiet, they were doing a terrible job of it, stomping across the ground, breaking branches, and crunching through leaves. But it was the "he might hear us" part that got my attention. Was the *he* they were talking about *me?* I didn't know how it could be since I'd just arrived myself. But I wasn't taking any chances.

As quietly as I could, I dropped to the ground. Imagining a group of ogres hungry for the taste of human flesh, I crawled toward the voices.

"Right here," said the voice of the leader.

I raised my head and was glad to see they weren't ogres, just three men in dark clothing with hats pulled low over their eyes. My relief didn't last for long though. The man in the middle, with broad shoulders and a big gut, was holding what looked like a really long rifle. A tall, pale guy also had a gun, and a shorter guy with a pointy nose gripped a shovel.

"I'll go that way. You head over to that rock." The leader slurred his words as though he'd been drinking. "And you hide behind the big tree down yonder. Soon as he comes through, we got 'im."

As the man with the shovel and the tall one started toward me, I realized my predicament. Even if they weren't after me, they'd completely blocked my path to the road. And if I didn't move quickly, I was going to be trapped.

"Think he's really got it?" asked Shorty as he headed toward the tree.

"He's got it." Long-tall-and-ugly nodded, heading to the rock on my right.

Knowing I wouldn't be able to crawl away in time, I got to my feet. A twig snapped under my heel, and the tall guy with the gun looked up from the spot where he'd been crouching.

"That you, Joe?"

Joe? I backed away slowly, hoping he couldn't see me as well as I could see him.

"Come out and give us a share o' that treasure," cackled Shorty. He was closing in on my left.

I didn't know what treasure they were talking about, but I knew I had to make a break for it fast. My only chance of escape was going back the way I'd come. But just then I heard something racing up behind me.

The two men in front of me didn't seem to hear it. They were both still peering into the dark trying to find me. The one with the shovel held it high above his head as though he was expecting to brain someone.

I looked from left to right. There was no way past them. But whatever was behind me was coming up fast. The footsteps were quieter than the men around me, but I could tell whatever was coming was big. I could hear it breathing heavily as it got closer and closer.

Just then, the tall goon turned his head. "I hear 'im," he whispered. He raised the gun over his head and ran straight at me.

Have you ever bumped into somebody at a party or the mall and thought, I know you. Then you realize you don't. You haven't met them before. And yet they still look really familiar. It's not until the next day, or the one after, that you suddenly realize who they looked like. But by then it's too late.

CHAPTER 8

The events that took place next were hard to keep track of. Even though I could see well enough in the dark, things were moving too fast, and it was still difficult for me to believe this was all real.

"I see 'im," Shorty yelled. He started toward me, swinging the shovel over his shoulder like a baseball bat. But just then, there was a shout and the sound of a scuffle. Shorty paused, and looked to his left. "You all right?" he shouted.

"He got past me!" called the leader. He sounded like he'd gotten the wind knocked out of him. "He's coming your way."

I turned to run, but the tall dude was right there. His eyes gleamed in his powder-white face as he raised his gun. "Where is it?" he said, revealing a mouth full of brown teeth.

"I don't know what you're talking about!" I screamed. "You have the wrong guy."

Either he didn't believe me or he didn't care. With a heavy grunt, he swung the butt of the rifle forward and down. I should have ducked, or at least tried to move out of the way, but I think a part of me was convinced this really was a dream and I was about to snap out of it. Instead I looked up in amazement as the heavy wooden stock swung toward my head. With my improved vision, I could make out the tiny grains of the wood. I wondered if it would hurt when it bit into my skull or if I'd wake up before I could feel it.

When I finally realized my head was about to be bashed in, it was too late to do anything but wince. Just before the gun connected, a hand reached out and caught it. I heard a sickening crunch, one that was way too familiar from my years of playing football. I knew the hand that had stopped the weapon either had broken bones or severely dislocated fingers. The guy was tough, though. The hand holding the stock of the gun shoved it backward into the chest of Long-tall-and-ugly, knocking him to the ground.

"Look out!" called the person behind me.

I turned in time to see Shorty coming straight at me. His shovel was in mid-swing. The only chance I had was to reach him before he reached me. Dropping into a classic tackling stance, I lowered my shoulder and charged. Apparently he didn't expect that. His eyes went wide as I met him square in the chest and lifted him off his feet. The shovel slipped out of his hands and went flying into the trees. I slammed him to the ground with a satisfying thud and thought, *I bet you don't run my way next time.*

Kneeling on the ground, I looked up to see who'd saved my bacon. He was tall and broad-shouldered. His arms bulged beneath his white undershirt. He looked like he'd make a good tight end. A broad-brimmed hat was pulled low over his face, so it was hard to see his features. But I could see his white teeth as he grinned. "Nice hit," he said.

I nodded dumbly. Something about the man was so familiar. I was sure I hadn't met him before, and yet I could swear I'd seen him. He flexed his left hand. I could see the thumb sticking out at an awkward angle. In his right hand, he held what looked like a long-sleeved shirt wrapped around some kind of bundle. It seemed heavy.

"Are you okay?" I asked.

Before he could answer, the leader of the group shouted. "Samuel, Johnny-boy, did you get 'im?"

The third man appeared to have gotten his wind back. I could see him coming closer, still holding his rifle. He hadn't spotted us in the cover of the trees yet, but it wouldn't be long until he got close enough to see his friends moaning on the ground.

"You better go," whispered the man with the bag. "There may be more of them out there." He stared down at me a moment longer, and something in his gaze made my heart pound. Why did he look so familiar? "That was a fine hit you put on that fellow," he said. "I'd like to see what you could do with a stick." Then he was running off into the trees, limping a little on one leg and clutching the bundle to his chest.

"Hey there," shouted the man with the rifle.

I turned to see him only a few yards away.

"Sucker hit me from behind," moaned the tall man, rolling back and forth on the ground.

The leader's eyes went wide. His raised the barrel of his gun.

It was too late to do anything but run. With no idea of where I was going, or even what direction I was heading in, I raced into the trees.

"Hold it right there!" a voice yelled.

I ducked behind a tree and slanted away from the men, hoping it was too dark for them to see me. A shot rang out and something slammed into my back, knocking me to the ground.

I jumped to my feet and kept running.

"There he goes!" another voice yelled. It was further away.

I began to sprint, knowing no one could catch me if I had a head start. But something was wrong with my left arm. There was a dull ache in my shoulder, and it was hard to move it. When I looked down at my chest, a hot ball of acid burned in my stomach, and I knew I was going to be sick. The front of my shirt was covered in blood.

□　　□　　□

Without any warning, my legs collapsed out from under me. I fell to the ground and turned my head just in time to keep from throwing up on myself. I touched the front of my chest with my right hand, and my fingers came away sticky.

This wasn't a dream then. When you get shot in dreams, you wake up. But I was still here. I could feel something hot and wet drip into the waistband of my pants.

That's my blood, I thought. *I've actually been shot.* The idea was so crazy, I might have laughed if I hadn't been in such pain. I could imagine myself returning to Brother Mortensen and saying, "I don't have a note. But does this hole in my chest count?" Would my mom still give me a hard time if I called her from the hospital?

I knew they were stupid thoughts, but I couldn't seem to clear my brain. I started to feel cold, and it was hard keeping my head up. *Going to faint,* I thought, when I heard the voices shouting again. They were getting closer—probably following the trail of my blood. It wasn't hard to imagine what they'd do if they found me laid out on the ground when they got here.

I had to get up. I grabbed the trunk of a nearby tree and pulled myself to my feet. My hand left a dark smear. The sight of it made me start to feel faint again, but I had to keep moving. I could hear the men clearly now. The one I thought of as Shorty said, "Careful, there's five or six of 'em, and they have guns."

"Shut up," said the leader, followed by the sound of a slap that made me smile through my pain. I wasn't sure I'd survive this, but Shorty wouldn't be doing any jumping jacks tomorrow.

Then I was running through the trees again. The ground dropped out from under me, and I managed to keep my footing for five or six steps, flailing my hands like I was trying to stop myself from going out of bounds before I reached the end zone. Then my boot caught on something and I was falling—rolling, bouncing, tumbling—my shoulder jolting in pain each time I landed on it.

I found myself lying on the wet grass behind a wooden fence. At first I didn't think I could stand up. My legs felt rubbery, like the time I got a concussion in a peewee football game when I was ten. But the men must have heard me fall. They had to be right behind me. I pulled myself over the fence and stumbled across an empty field of plowed soil.

"Hurry up," my coach shouted. "Safety's coming up your back." I tried to juke to the right, but I didn't think my legs obeyed me.

"I told you to be home by eight," my mom said. I thought she'd be mad at me, but instead she wrapped an arm around my good shoulder and helped me forward.

"How many times have I told you to avoid getting shot on a quarterback option?" my dad asked, grabbing my other arm. I knew they couldn't really be there. But I was willing to take any help I could get.

I thought I saw a light in the distance. I tried to lift my head from my chest and found I couldn't. Then I was out of the field. My feet hit hard-packed dirt.

"Hold it right there!" someone shouted. I rolled my eyes forward to see a man with a gun pointed at me. They'd found me after all.

"Put your hands in the air," he called.

I tried to tell him my hands wouldn't do what I told them to. All that came out of my mouth was a mumble that made no sense, even to me.

"He's been shot," a voice cried. It was high-pitched. A woman or a girl.

I tried to take a step forward and found myself lying face-first in the dirt.

The man with the gun walked forward, his boots stopping right by my head. "Got a hole in you, sure enough. Well, let's see if we can get you inside before you bleed everything in you."

He wrapped his hands around my chest, and I couldn't help howling as a burning pain roared through my body.

He said something that sounded like, "If you can scream like that, you probably won't die tonight." But I was beyond listening. I could feel myself losing consciousness. Just before I did, I glanced up at the window of a small, one-story house. There was a girl standing at the window. She was holding a lamp of some kind. The flame illuminated her face.

She was beautiful.

I was sitting in the back of seminary, goofing around with Jeff Greene, when Brother Mortensen looked my way.

"Brother Steele," he said, pointing a small black rod in my direction. "Would you care to tell us what this is?"

"It's a key," I tried to say. But instead the word that came out of my mouth was, "Knowledge."

"Very good." He beamed.

Beside me, Jeff whispered, "Suck up."

I blinked, and it wasn't Brother Mortensen standing in front of the class anymore. Instead it was the man I'd seen in the woods—the one who kept me from getting a nasty club-shaped dent in my head. He was wearing an old-fashioned-looking suit with a floppy bow tie. A lock of light brown hair poked out from the front of his brown felt hat.

He stared at me with blue eyes I couldn't seem to turn away from and asked, "Do you know who I am?"

I knew I should. He looked so familiar. But I couldn't remember for the life of me. An actor maybe? Or one of my teachers from elementary school? No. But who?

Jeff shook his head at me, grinned, and mouthed, "Loser."

The answer was right on the tip of my tongue when a girl with blonde, curly hair raised her hand. "I know," she said.

I leaned forward to hear her answer, but just as she started to speak, I woke up.

CHAPTER 9

I rolled over in bed, blinked at the sunlight streaming into the room, and waited for my mom to come pull the covers off me. She gives me one warning before yanking me out of my warm cocoon. If that doesn't work, I know a cold glass of water in the face is next. Pulling the blankets *always* works.

When she didn't come in after a couple of minutes, I sat up and rubbed my eyes. I tried to remember if it was a school day or the weekend. I reached for my alarm clock to see what time it was, and my fingers touched something thin and waxy.

"You're awake." A little woman bustled into the room. If I hadn't been completely awake before, I was now. She wasn't anyone I knew, and she definitely wasn't my mom. She had long dark hair and was wearing a flowered dress so long it nearly touched the floor.

I looked around, trying to remember where I was and how I got here. I was sitting on a tall bed with even taller posts at each of the four corners. Beside the bed was a night table with a hairbrush and a long white candle in a metal holder. On the other side of the bed was a dresser with a blue pitcher and bowl. There was a doll beside the pitcher.

There was something odd about the room that I couldn't put my finger on. Before I could figure out what it was, though, the woman set a steaming plate on the bedspread in front of me, and all thoughts disappeared as I saw eggs, ham, and two thick slices of brown bread with melting butter.

"I thought you might be hun—" she started.

Before she could finish speaking, I was shoving a forkful of eggs into my mouth, followed by a huge bite of some of the best bread I'd ever tasted. I couldn't remember ever being this hungry. The smell of fried ham brought saliva to the corner of my mouth.

"Oh, my," the woman said as I cut off a huge slice of meat and shoved it into my mouth.

"Sorry," I managed to get out around another bite of bread. The butter slathered across it was so good I could have eaten that all by itself. "Really . . . hungry."

"You go right ahead," she said, folding her arms across her chest. "I like to see a man eat."

I hoped that was true, because for a few minutes I couldn't seem to do anything *but* eat. I couldn't remember what day it was or where I was, but the food was so amazing it didn't seem to matter.

"That was so-o-o-o good," I moaned as I sopped up the rest of the egg with my last bite of bread.

She nodded with a pleased smile and took the plate. "There's more if you're still hungry."

I shook my head. My stomach was quiet for the moment, and my brain was starting to take control again. "Thanks. That was amazing. But if you don't mind me asking, who are you? And where am I? How did I get here?"

Her lips pulled up in a smile and her eyes flashed. She looked like the kind of woman who spent a lot of time smiling. "I could ask the same of you. But since you're the guest, I'll go first. I'm Phoebe Jagger. And you're in my daughter's bedroom."

"Daughter?" I looked around, suddenly aware of the pink curtains and flowered bedspread.

Phoebe chuckled. "Jennie graciously offered up her bed when my husband found you in our side field with a bullet wound."

It all came back at once. The party, the tunnels, the door, the man with the gun.

"What day is it?" I asked.

"Saturday."

How could that be? The sun had been setting when I finally escaped from the tunnels the night before—which had to be Saturday night, didn't it? That would make today Sunday. Only it didn't feel like two days had passed. I looked out the window where the grass was still wet with morning dew. Somehow I'd lost a day—or gained one. My head spun. But I didn't have time to worry about that now. If it really *was* Saturday morning . . . I still had time.

"I've got to go," I shouted, throwing back the blankets and jumping out of bed. "I've got to get to a football game!"

Across the bed from me, the woman's face went pink and she quickly looked at the floor.

I glanced down at myself and realized I was only wearing my boxers and a big white bandage around my shoulder. "I . . . ah . . . where . . . ?" I could feel my cheeks heat up as I noticed the open door, and remembered the daughter.

The woman pointed toward a wooden chair with my shirt and jacket hanging from the back. My pants were folded on the seat of the chair, and my boots and socks were on the floor. She gave me a quick peek before dropping her eyes again, and I could swear I saw her grinning. "I did my best to get out the blood."

I shuffled awkwardly over to the chair, trying to keep my hands strategically placed, and grabbed my pants. In lightning-fast time, I pulled on the pants, shirt, and boots. "Can I use your phone?" I asked, taking the jacket.

"Phone?" the woman asked with a puzzled look on her face.

"Your telephone. I have to call my parents. I have a football game in a couple of hours, and they're probably totally freaking out."

The woman stared at me like I was crazy. But I didn't have time to worry about that. I stepped through the door into what appeared to be a combination kitchen and living room. "Would it be possible to get a ride into . . ."

I stopped and looked slowly around the room. Suddenly I realized why the bedroom seemed so odd. Something was missing. There were no lights, no stereos, no clock radios, no TVs, no computers. There weren't even any electrical outlets as far as I could see. Instead of a microwave and toaster, the kitchen had a big iron sink with what looked like a hand pump, and an antique metal stove. In front of the stone fireplace was a spinning wheel that could have come straight out of a museum or . . . or out of the prop shop above Ladan's office.

"You're part of it, aren't you?" I asked, turning to the woman.

"Part of . . . what?" She was no longer smiling. In fact, she looked a little scared. I wasn't buying her act. This had Ladan written all over it.

"Look," I said, holding out my hands, "I don't know what he told you about me, Mrs. Jagger. Or what he said I did. But whatever it is, I don't deserve to be put through something like this. I'm done playing his game."

The woman edged slowly away from me. "Maybe you'd better go." She glanced to her right, and I saw an old-fashioned pistol lying on a shelf.

"Yeah. I'm leaving, right now." I shrugged. "I'm sorry he got you involved in this, but thanks for the breakfast. It really was great."

I lunged for the door. It took me a minute to figure out how to use the metal latch, and all the time I was fiddling with it, I kept expecting a shot in the back. The woman seemed nice enough, but after last night I thought Ladan might be capable of anything.

When I finally got the door open, I stumbled across the

front porch and into the yard. Sitting only a few feet away from me was a girl in a bonnet and a dress that looked a lot like the other woman's. She looked up at me, and I realized I'd seen her before. She was the girl I'd seen looking out the window the night before—the one with the lamp. There was also something familiar about her, but I couldn't remember what.

The girl was sitting on a one-legged stool, plunging a wooden handle up and down in a barrel. I recognized the handle and the barrel it went into at once. It was a butter churn, just like the one I'd seen the girl in the prop store using. If that wasn't proof this was Ladan's doing, I didn't know what was.

"Jennie, look out." Mrs. Jagger stepped out onto the porch. She was holding the antique pistol in both hands. "Get into the house," she called. "This man's dangerous."

"Don't shoot!" I said, holding up my hands.

The girl with the butter churn looked me up and down. A chicken pecked at something near her foot, and she shooed it aside. "He doesn't look dangerous."

"I'm not," I said. "I just need to get back to town. Can I borrow your car?"

The girl gave me the same look her mother had when I'd asked to use their phone.

"See," Mrs. Jagger said, still pointing the gun at me. "That's what I mean. There's something wrong with him. He's talking crazy. He asked if he could use my fawn and said he was late for something called foot-bowl!"

"You're not from around here, are you?" the girl asked me.

I sighed. "Right now, I don't even know where *here* is."

Mrs. Jagger moved around until she was standing between her daughter and me. "My husband's right out back. He'll be here any minute."

"He is not," the girl said. "He went to fetch the doctor." She stood up—letting the stool drop to the ground—and pushed the gun so it was no longer pointing directly at me. "You can put your hands down."

I lowered my arms, still keeping an eye on the gun. The girl might think I was okay, but her mother clearly wasn't convinced.

"I don't think he should be here with your father gone," Mrs. Jagger whispered.

The girl shook her head, the curly blonde hair poking out from her bonnet bouncing around like little springs. She smiled at me, and I tried to smile back, although it was hard to with the gun still in her mother's hands. "He must have hit his head last night, Mother. He's not dangerous. He's just addled."

I've heard lots of pick-up lines. "What's a good-looking girl like you doing without a date tonight?" "If I work hard on my mission, can I come back to a girl like you?" "I must have dreamed about you because you look like a dream come true." Some of them work. Most of them don't. But I'm pretty sure the way to meet a girl isn't by convincing her you're nuts.

CHAPTER 10

"I'm not crazy," I said, although at this point I wasn't entirely sure of that.

"Of course not," said the girl, who I figured had to be Jennie, since she seemed to be the only daughter there. "You probably just bumped your head last night. You're confused." She took her mother by the elbow and led her onto the porch. "Come back inside with us."

I couldn't argue that I wasn't confused. That was for sure. But I couldn't stand around either. "I have to get into town."

"The doctor can take you," Jennie said. "He should be here with Papa any minute."

It might be good to meet with a doctor. And since I had no idea where "town" was, a ride would be good, too. Jennie stood holding the door open, until I relented and went back inside.

"Can I get you a cup of water?" she asked, hanging her bonnet from a peg just inside the door.

"That would be great," I said. Mrs. Jagger set the pistol

back on the shelf, but I noticed she sat in a rocking chair within arm's length of the gun. I took a wooden bench by the fireplace. Jennie took a tin cup from a cupboard and began pumping the metal arm over the sink. Soon, clear fresh water was running from the pump.

"Not to be rude," I said, waving my arm at the antiques, "but what's with all this stuff? Are you, what do you call it, Amish or something?"

Mrs. Jagger stiffened noticeably, and sniffed. "We're Methodist. Three generations."

"Oh, sorry." I tried to think of what I knew about Methodists. I had a couple of friends who I was pretty sure were Methodists, and I think I would have noticed if they didn't believe in using modern appliances. Maybe it was better if I just kept my mouth shut while I waited.

"Where are you from?" Jennie asked as she handed me my water and sat on a bench across the room.

The water tasted cold and wonderful. "West Jordan," I said, wiping my mouth with the back of my hand.

"Jordan." For the first time since I'd asked to use her phone, Mrs. Jagger seemed to warm up a little. "My sister-in-law lives there. Temperance and Levi Barrows. Have you heard of them?"

I shook my head, not bothering to mention that I would have remembered a couple named Temperance and Levi.

"I suppose you came by canal boat," she said.

Canal boat? Now who was the crazy one? "No. I drove to Salt Lake and apparently walked from there."

"Salt Lake?" Jennie pronounced the city slowly, as if she'd never heard of it before. She looked from me to her mother, and I was pretty sure they were passing some kind of message between them. "I'm afraid I've never heard of that town."

"Are you serious?" I asked. Who hadn't heard of Salt Lake? Something was wrong, but I wasn't sure what. Then a thought occurred to me. "This is going to sound crazy, but where are we? What city?"

"Palmyra," Jennie and her mother said at once.

"You're kidding." Palmyra was a little town down by Spanish Fork. We played the Spanish Fork Dons every year. "How did I get here? That's, like, fifty miles south of West Jordan."

"You mean west," Jennie said with a sympathetic smile. "Jordon is fifty miles *east* of us. Right along the canal. That's why my mother thought you must have come by boat."

Something didn't add up. Fifty miles west of West Jordan there was nothing but desert. And we weren't in the desert. In fact, it didn't really seem like we were in Utah at all. I couldn't think of a single place anywhere in the state that had rolling hills or woods like the ones I'd walked through.

Then one of those weird connections hit. One where all of the pieces suddenly fall into place, but the whole doesn't make any more sense than the parts do. I'd heard of only one other Palmyra, and there was no way I could be there. "What state are we in?" I asked, dreading the answer.

Jennie laughed. Not in a mean way, but the way you'd

laugh at a three-year-old struggling to tie his shoes. "You really are confused, poor thing. We're in New York, of course."

For a moment I could only sit there in shock. What she was telling me was impossible. And yet, it added up with what I'd seen. The woods. The rolling hills. I'd known I wasn't in Utah as soon as I walked out the door, but I hadn't let my mind accept the fact. I'd never been to New York in my life. My family had visited Palmyra one summer to see the Hill Cumorah Pageant, but I had stayed home for a football camp.

Which meant I *had* been drugged somehow. Drugged and flown completely across the country. How and why, I had no idea. But that also explained all the old stuff. I looked around at the cabin, nodding. Props, all of it. When my family had gone to the pageant, they'd visited the Smith family farm, and before that, stopped at Nauvoo. My brother had told me how they had old buildings set up, complete with actors to show you how life was back in the pioneer days.

"So this is what—some kind of historical exhibit?"

Jennie gave her mom another one of those looks. "I'm not sure I understand what you're talking about."

"All these antiques," I said, wondering why they were still trying to play games with me. "The butter churn, the gas lamps, the spinning wheel, the pump. Even this house. It's to show people what it was like back in the 1800s. Right?"

Jennie gave me another look. But this one wasn't amused. It was the kind of look you give someone who's dying and the disease may be contagious. "Maybe you better lie down."

"Come on," I said. "You can cut it out. The game's over."

Jennie swallowed. "What year do you think it is?"

Now I had to laugh. "What year do *you* think it is?"

"Eighteen twenty-seven." She said it so seriously I could almost convince myself she believed it.

"Good one," I said, shaking my head. "I'm in Palmyra, New York, and it's eighteen twenty-seven. Next I guess you'll tell me the guy I saw up on the hill with the bag was Joseph Smith."

Just then the door banged open, and two men stepped into the room. One was dressed in clothes a lot like my own. He had weathered brown skin and shaggy hair. The other looked like an actor in an old movie. He was dressed in a fancy white jacket with blue-and-white striped pants. He was wearing a black top hat and carrying a large leather bag.

The man with the shaggy hair took a step toward me and asked in a stern voice, "What's this about Joe Smith?"

◻   ◻   ◻

"Papa!" Jennie jumped up from the bench and wrapped her arms around the neck of the shaggy-haired man.

He hugged her back before hanging his hat from a peg on the wall.

"Feeling a little better, are you?" the man asked me. I guessed he must have been the one who'd rescued me the night before.

"Yes, sir," I said, with a nod.

Mrs. Jagger frowned, and Jennie bit her lip. "He's a little confused. We think he must have gotten a bump on the head last night."

"Is that right?" asked the man in the top hat. He set his bag on the wooden floor. "What's your name, son?"

"Kaleo Steele," I said.

"Kaleo? What kind of name's that?" asked Mr. Jagger.

"It's Hawaiian," I said. "My mother's from the island of Lanai."

"Really?" asked the man with the top hat. "How fascinating." He stuck out his hand. "Dr. Gain Robinson."

"Good to meet you," I said, shaking his hand. He was dressed kind of strangely, but at least he wasn't shooting at me or calling me crazy.

"So what's this about Joe Smith?" Mr. Jagger asked again, scowling. "You one of them fools up in the hills last night searching for that boy's so-called gold Bible?"

I looked at the doctor, hoping he'd tell these people they were nuts. But he looked just as sincere and interested as the rest of them. I didn't want to call them all liars, but the idea that I had somehow traveled back in time was crazier than everything else that had happened to me put together. I decided to stick to the facts—without mentioning the weird stuff like the tunnels and the letter.

"No, sir," I said. "I got lost and I was trying to find my way back to town. I accidentally ran into three guys, and one of them shot me. I was trying to get away and I ended up here."

"Humph," snorted Mr. Jagger. "Thought I heard someone messing around up there in the woods. Old Liver Spots was barking up a storm."

"And you suffered a blow to the head?" asked Dr. Robinson.

"Not that I remember. There was a guy, short with a pointy nose, that tried to brain me with a club."

"Johnny Viggers," Jennie said and from the tone of her voice, it was clear she didn't think much of him.

"But someone stopped him," I said. "A big guy with broad shoulders. He was carrying a bag and running. I think maybe the other men were looking for him. I heard them say something about treasure."

Mrs. Jagger frowned, and Mr. Jagger opened his mouth as if he was going to say something, but the doctor spoke first. "We'll get to your head in a moment. Right now I want to take a look at that shoulder. Abel here tells me you lost quite a bit of blood last night."

I hadn't thought about my gunshot wound all morning. In fact, I hadn't felt any pain at all. Now as I looked down at my coat and saw the nickel-sized round hole through it and through my shirt, a terrible thought occurred to me.

"Is this what you were wearing last night?" the doctor said, fingering the hole. "Can't see any blood on it at all."

"I washed it myself," said Mrs. Jagger.

"I'm feeling much better now," I said. "In fact, I don't think you even need to take a look at it."

"Nonsense," he said. "Remove your jacket and shirt."

I remembered what had happened to my cuts and blisters the night before. I hadn't thought about it when Mrs. Jagger said she'd done the best she could to clean the blood out of my clothes, but now I realized there was no way she could have gotten them this clean. And there was no way I should feel this good the morning after getting shot.

"Really," I said, trying to pull free. "I'm fine."

But the doctor was already tugging back my coat and lowering the shoulder of my shirt. "Too bashful to let a couple of beautiful young ladies see your bare chest?"

He slid the bandage gently off my shoulder, opened his mouth to say something, and then just stared. The entire room was silent.

Everyone was looking at my shoulder. But I didn't want to. I already knew what I would see. Still, I couldn't help my gaze from drifting down. Except for being a little pinker than the surrounding skin, the spot on my shoulder where I'd been shot was unmarked. The bullet hole was gone.

A witness is a person who sees or hears something. If you are a witness to a crime, it means you saw it occur. If you are a witness to an event, it means you were there when it happened. Why would a man who was blind—who couldn't see a crime or an event if it took place in front of his nose—call himself a witness? And why would he call me one when the only thing I wanted to see was my own front door?

CHAPTER 11

I s this some kind of joke?" Dr. Robinson prodded the pink spot on my chest, leaned me forward, and checked my back. He turned to Mr. Jagger. "I thought you said this boy had been shot."

Mr. Jagger pushed the doctor out of the way. "Let me see." He stuck a finger through the hole in my shirt and jacket, then stared at me like a frog on a dissecting table. "You're one of them, aren't you?"

"One of what?" I asked, wishing everyone would just leave me alone.

"One of those foreigners." Mr. Jagger stepped back, rubbing his hands on his pants, as if he'd just touched something nasty.

"He said he was from Jordan." Mrs. Jagger leaned toward the gun.

"I ain't never heard of no Steeles in Jordan," Mr. Jagger said. "And I ain't never heard of no Kaleo neither."

Dr. Robinson stepped back as I pulled up my shirt and coat. "I'm sure there's a reasonable explanation. Perhaps he wasn't shot at all. Perhaps he got the blood on him from someone else?"

"How do you explain the holes in the front and back of his shirt then?" Mr. Jagger scowled at me.

I didn't have any explanation.

"He's one of them, I tell you." Mr. Jagger turned to the doctor. "'Bout a week ago, three foreigners come through town, poking around and asking questions. Called themselves nee-fights."

"Nephites?" The word escaped my lips before I could stop it.

"That's right, *Nephites*."

"What does that have to do with this boy?" Dr. Robinson asked.

"I hired all three to help me build a fence." Mr. Jagger's eyes narrowed. "One of 'em cut his arm pretty bad with a two-handed saw. Figured he was gonna lose it for sure. But by lunch he was good as new. Black magic, I called it. And that's what I call it now. I fired those three Nephites that very day. And I don't want this fourth one on my property a minute longer."

The Three Nephites? I couldn't believe what I was hearing. The Three Nephites were here, and they were building fences? What did that mean?

Mr. Jagger held open his door and pointed out into the

yard. "I want you out of my house. I let you spend the night under my roof. Probably be cursed for it, too."

"I'll take him into town," Dr. Robinson said.

"I don't care what you do with him." Mr. Jagger lifted his upper lip in a snarl.

I started toward the door, feeling like the lowest of low-down mutts. I glanced toward Jennie, wondering if she hated me too. Her mother seemed terrified of me, her father clearly hated me, but she was looking at me with . . . what? Curiosity? Interest?

"Out!" Mr. Jagger shoved me in the back, and I staggered across the front porch, barely keeping from falling.

"Climb on up in my carriage," Dr. Robinson said. "I'll take you back to town. It's only a couple of miles."

A couple of miles? If I'd known a town was that close, I could have run back.

The doctor snapped his reins, and a pair of matched black horses started forward. I looked at the doctor's black leather bag, his clothes, and his carriage, and realized Jennie hadn't been lying.

"It really is," I murmured under my breath.

"Really is what?" the doctor asked.

"Eighteen twenty-seven."

He looked at me and laughed. "For another three months."

Wait, three? "What's the date?"

"September twenty-ninth," he said. "Usually I try to take Saturdays off. I'm not getting any younger, you know."

September 29, 1827. That date meant something. But

what? I thought back to last night and the man I'd seen. The one on the hill. It really was him. September 1827 was when . . . "Joseph Smith found the gold plates."

The doctor looked over at me sharply. "What did you say?"

I swallowed. "Nothing. It's just . . . I think the man I saw on the hill last night—the one who saved me—was Joseph Smith."

"Could be. The Smith place is just up the road on the right."

"You know them?" I asked. This was so weird. Joseph Smith. I'd seen him in person without even knowing it.

Dr. Robinson nodded. "My nephew Alexander and I have treated their family since they moved here. Joe Jr. was only a little fellow at the time. Eleven or twelve, I guess. Had to use crutches after an operation on his leg to cut out a piece of bone."

I remember that story, I nearly said, before realizing I'd have no way of explaining how I could know about it. "What's he like?" I asked instead.

"Good people," Dr. Robinson said. "High character. Hard workers." He rubbed his chin. "You're new to the area. Some folks have some mean and spiteful things to say about the Smith family. Calling them shiftless and treasure seekers. Liars and cheats. There's some pretty odd talk about a solid gold book and angels. I imagine if you did run into Joe last night, the fellows you ran into were looking for that gold."

That didn't make sense. The Book of Mormon wasn't real. Joseph Smith made it up. There really were no gold plates. So what was he doing running through the forest at night with a bag? Especially if he knew people were looking for him. But if the Book of Mormon wasn't real, who were the people calling themselves the Three Nephites? It was way too confusing.

For a while we rode in silence. Occasionally we'd pass another carriage going the other direction, and the doctor would wave. And once we passed a huge boat of a wagon pulled by four sets of oxen.

On the right, I spotted a two-story frame house with white siding. I leaned out of the carriage, trying to get a better look. "Is that . . . ?"

He nodded. "A while back they came to me for help with a legal matter concerning the land agent. I wrote that I had full confidence in them. An hour later that petition had sixty more signatures. I don't know about any angels or whatnot, but they are good folk. Poor as church mice, but good."

In a field that looked like it had been recently cleared, a group of kids were laughing and running around. One of them was holding a stick. He swung it and hit something into the air. A man in a blue shirt ran to the edge of the field, raised his hand, and caught it to the wild cheers of the children. Was that the Prophet playing baseball?

"Is it true?" the doctor asked.

"What?" I looked away from the game.

"Are you one of them? Are you a fourth Nephite?"

I thought about it. The letter from Ladan had been signed "From one witness to another." I guessed that in a sense the Three Nephites were witnesses—witnesses as the last days unfolded, until the return of Christ. Except they weren't real, I had to remind myself. There were no Nephites. They were a figment of Joseph Smith's imagination.

I shook my head. "No. I'm not."

"Oh." The doctor looked disappointed. "It's just that I didn't tell Abel Jagger, but I met one of them as well. About two weeks ago. We had dinner together."

"You had dinner with one of the Three Nephites?"

"I did," Dr. Robinson said. "We discussed history over a plate of mutton and potatoes. He was quite knowledgeable on the subject—history, not mutton. Which was quite amazing, considering that he was blind."

"Ladan?"

He nodded. "You *do* know him, then?"

I couldn't believe it. Ladan—the man I'd talked with the day before—had dinner with this man more than two hundred years before. It made my mind reel. "Yes, I know him. In fact, he's the reason I'm here."

The doctor snapped open his bag and pulled out an envelope. Unlike the one I'd found in my jacket, this one looked brand-new, but the wax seal was the same. Three Ns. For the Three Nephites?

My name wasn't on the front of this one. Did that mean he didn't know who it was for at the time? Or was it something else?

"He said I should keep it," the doctor said. "Until I met a young man seeking knowledge. He called the person I should give the envelope to 'the fourth Nephite.' Are you sure that's not you?"

I thought about the first message. *Knowledge is the key, and faith the power to turn it.* I didn't think I had any faith, but I was in desperate need of knowledge. I pulled the first envelope out of my coat pocket and showed the doctor the seal on the back. "I guess it is me."

"Good." He handed me the envelope.

We turned right, and what had been quiet countryside was suddenly a busy street filled with people walking, talking, riding, and shouting. "Main Street," he said. "This used to be a pretty small place, but ever since the canal came through, it's been growing like a colt."

I could see what he meant. Buildings seemed to be going up everywhere. The strangest thing, though, was the city itself. It didn't look like any city I'd ever seen before. The streets were dirt. Dust kicked up everywhere from carts, horses, even a few sheep. Along each side of the road were shops with big glass windows. And in front of the shops were wooden sidewalks. It looked a lot like one of those towns you see in old Western movies.

"Where are you staying?" he asked.

I had no idea.

He pointed to a three-story building—the tallest in town from what I could see. "If you're looking for a hotel, I recommend the Eagle. Good rooms at a fair price and a hot bath." He winked. "You look like you could use one."

I didn't tell him I had no money and no idea how I was going to get some.

He pulled the reins and clicked his tongue twice. The horses stopped in front of the hotel. "Good luck, son." He held out his hand. I shook it, suddenly wishing he wouldn't leave just yet.

I looked up at him. "You said you believe the Smiths are honest people."

He nodded.

"But you don't believe Joseph Smith really saw an angel like he said, do you?"

The doctor looked down the street. "There are plenty of churchgoing folk in this town—Methodists, Baptists, Presbyterians, and others. Chapels are springing up like wildflowers. What young Joseph has been saying has ruffled a lot of feathers. Some folks around here don't look too kindly on the man or his family lately—especially the religious folks. And many of those folks are my patients. I guess it makes me weak, but if I were to believe in angels and gold Bibles, I'd lose a lot of my business." Then he looked back at me. "But just between you and me, I think he might be telling the truth. At least he thinks he is. Don't know if you feel the same way or not, seeing as how you only met the man for a minute and I've known him a good part of his life, but if you do believe, I'd be careful about who you tell that to. Or you could find yourself involved in things you don't want to be a part of."

With that, he clicked his tongue and the horses started down the street again.

"Be careful about who you tell that to," he'd said. I didn't need to be told twice. I had the feeling I'd be keeping a lot of things to myself until I could figure out how to get home.

I looked up at the hotel, wondering what I was going to do. As I stepped out of the street onto the wooden sidewalk, I bumped into someone heading the other direction.

"Look where you're going," he growled.

"Sorry." I turned to find Long-tall-and-ugly frowning at me. I recognized him and his two friends from the night before. All except the leader looked like they'd had a hard night, and even he didn't look happy. Fortunately the tall one didn't seem to know who I was. The night had been dark, and he hadn't gotten a good look at my face. Unfortunately, Shorty—the only one who had seen me up close—glanced over his shoulder as the trio walked past.

I turned away as fast as I could, looking for a door to duck into. Before I could, Shorty elbowed the big guy in the side and whispered something. All three of them stopped and turned.

I needed to give the leader of these three jerks a name. I had Shorty for the one I'd tackled, and Long-tall-and-ugly for the guy who was, well, long, tall, and ugly. But I didn't have a name for their leader. "Leader" was giving him too much credit. He'd actually stayed in the back the night before, even though he was carrying a gun.

"Beer Belly" might work. He definitely had the belly and from the way he'd been slurring his words, he seemed to have had quite a bit to drink. But maybe his belly hadn't come from beer alone. Maybe he was addicted to pancakes, or mashed potatoes and gravy. "Pancake Belly" didn't have the same ring to it.

I'd have to work on it. Preferably, though, at a time when they weren't chasing me.

CHAPTER 12

"Hey, you!" The leader of the three—the one I hadn't come up with a name for yet—saw me first. He pointed a finger that looked like it hadn't been washed in a while and broke into an awkward jog. His boot heels rattled against the boardwalk.

Long-tall-and-ugly recognized me a second later. Shorty, in particular, seemed anxious to meet me. I noticed with more than a little satisfaction that he was hunched over at an awkward-looking angle.

I didn't have any time to gloat, though. They were coming fast. I looked around, realized that I had to get off the street, and darted into the nearest door. It happened to be the lobby of the Eagle Hotel.

"Can I help you?" asked a man in a long black coat. With his stretched-out face and slicked-back hair, he looked like one of those guys you see running funeral homes.

I checked over my shoulder. The three guys were nearly

to the door. Would they try to come after me inside the hotel? I thought I could take one or two of them—I'd handled a lot tougher guys on the football field—but I wasn't sure Igor behind the desk would be much help.

I walked to the desk, waiting to hear if the door opened behind me.

"Hi," I said, sounding dumb even to myself.

"Did you wish to take lodging, sir?"

Sir. That was cool. I'd never been called sir before. I needed a room, but I had no way to pay for it. I'd left my wallet with my ID back in the storage room, and I didn't have any cash to speak of, or a credit card in my wallet, even if I'd had it with me. Then I remembered my cash wouldn't be any good here anyway. What would people in the 1800s say if you offered them a bill dated almost two hundred years in the future? And credit cards weren't even invented yet.

Igor looked over my shoulder and frowned. He waved both hands in a go-away gesture. I didn't have to look to see who he was motioning to, but I did anyway. The three jerks were standing just outside the glass door, glaring at me. I wondered if the hotel had some kind of back door.

"Your name?" the hotel guy asked, returning his attention to me.

"Kaleo Steele." I wondered how long I could keep the guy talking before he threw me out in the street. Probably not as long as the dudes behind me could wait.

Instead of kicking me out, though, the hotel guy beamed

like I was the mayor of the town. "Ah, Mr. Steele," he said. "You'll be staying with us for seven days."

"I will?"

He gave me an odd look, and I quickly nodded. "I mean, right. I will."

"Very good. Breakfast, lunch, and dinner are served in the dining room at eight, one, and six. Along with your meals, you are entitled to one hot bath. An additional bath will be two bits." He slid a metal key across the counter and turned a large leather book so it was facing me. "Sign here," he said, handing me a quill pen.

I signed my name on the line and gulped. "Um, how do I pay for all this?"

"It's been paid for," he said. "I thought you knew. A gentleman arranged for your stay last week."

Ladan. So he *did* know I was coming. But how could he have known long before I was born? Or did this mean that he could travel back in time too? It was totally confusing.

"Do you have any luggage?" the man asked.

"Uh, no." As I took the key, I couldn't help looking out at the men on the sidewalk and smirking. Apparently they didn't want to start anything inside the hotel. The leader lifted his upper lip and held out his finger, pretending to shoot a gun. I should have left it alone, but I couldn't help dropping my shoulder a little and pretending to make a tackle. Shorty's face went red.

I was sure I would run into them again, but for now, they couldn't touch me.

My room was on the second floor. Even though I knew

where—and when—I was, I still found myself looking for the TV remote and the phone. Of course there was no TV, no phone, no Internet connection, and no electric lights. The room was barely large enough to fit the metal bed and a small dresser with a pitcher of water and a bowl.

I walked to the window and had to convince myself I wasn't watching a TV show. Carriages rolled up and down the street, kicking up plumes of dust behind their spinning wooden wheels. Men in cowboy hats and long coats walked beside women in bonnets and long dresses. Across the street, a wooden sign read, "Vaughn's General Merchandise—Groceries, Cloth, Cutlery, and Notions." As far as I knew, a notion was like an idea.

If I'd still had any suspicions that this was all some big practical joke, they were gone now.

I dropped onto the bed and tore open the envelope Dr. Robinson had given me. Inside was a letter wrapped around a bunch of coins and bills like nothing I'd ever seen before. I tucked the money into my pocket and read the spiky writing. Like the first letter, it began with what sounded like a scripture.

"For every one that asketh receiveth; and he that seeketh findeth; and to him that knocketh it shall be opened."

Fat chance of that. I'd knocked, kicked, pounded, and yelled, and the door hadn't opened for me. As if reading my thoughts, the next part of the letter read:

Kaleo, the Lord doesn't always give us what we want. But if we ask of Him with real faith in the power of His hand, He will grant unto us that which we need most. The key is knowing what to ask for.

There it was again. The key. And with it, faith and knowledge. The problem was, I didn't have faith. Not really. I mean, when I was younger I got up and bore my testimony with the rest of the kids my age. But was that faith, or just repeating what everyone else said? And *knowledge*. The only thing I knew for sure was that I didn't know anything. It seemed like an impossible puzzle to solve—without faith I couldn't get knowledge, but I didn't know enough to have faith.

The last part of the letter didn't offer any help.

Get yourself some new clothes. Bullet holes are not in style, and I don't have much time for tailoring. You've followed my instructions twice. Your next message lies with the brother of the one you seek. Be Swift, time is running out.

From one witness to another,

Jadan

Somehow he had known I was going to get shot and that I'd end up here in this hotel. That should have made me feel better, but somehow the fact that the person running my life had intentionally sent me to take a bullet didn't inspire confidence.

I read over the letter again. *Your next message lies with the brother of one you seek.* That was real helpful, since as far as I knew, I wasn't seeking anyone. *Time is running out.* What was that supposed to mean? Was something going to happen? And what did he mean that I had followed his instructions twice? If this letter was supposed to be some kind of clue, I had no idea what it meant.

Something rattled around in the bottom of the envelope. I flipped it upside down and shook a tiny piece of metal out onto my palm. Turning it over in my fingers, I saw that there were two metal rectangles connected to a circular opening at the top. It sort of looked like the kind of charm you'd put on a bracelet, but it was made of the same dark metal as the tiny black rod I'd found with the first letter.

I peered into the hole of the charm and squinted. It was tough to tell in the dim light of the room, but it looked like there were groves inside. The same kind of grooves carved into the—

I nearly dropped the piece of metal as I realized what it was. With shaking hands, I searched my coat pockets for the envelope I'd found by the door. *Please tell me I didn't lose it!* No. There it was—crumpled in a ball. I pulled it from my coat and found the rod.

With the rod in my left hand, I slid the charm onto the end of it. It took a little twisting and turning, but soon it slid onto the rod—clicking in place about three quarters of the way down. I held the rod up toward the window.

"Ladan, you old dog," I whispered.

Knowledge is the key, he'd written. That might be true, but the rod was a key too. I was sure of it. All I needed to find were the rest of the pieces and slide them into place.

But where? I reread the letter. The only directions were to get myself some new clothes. The store across the street maybe?

Before I could go anywhere, though, I had to make a pit stop. This morning's huge breakfast was catching up with me. I looked around the room, realizing for the first time there was no bathroom. The bowl on the dresser had a hand towel beside it—so I guessed that was for washing. But where was the toilet? There were no doors off the room except for the one leading back into the hallway.

I stepped out into the hall, and nearly ran over a girl not much older than I was, carrying a handful of sheets. She paused. "Can I help you?"

I could barely understand her accent and felt my face go red.

"I was, um, just wondering . . . Where are the bathrooms?"

"You want to bathe?"

I shook my head, wishing she'd picked a different time to come by. "No. I just need to . . . Could you tell me where the toilets are?"

"Toilet?"

This was getting awkward. My stomach made a loud gurgling noise and I must have crossed my legs, because all at once her face went red as well. "Oh-h-h. The privy is out back." She stepped to the door of my room and pointed toward the bed. "The chamber pot is there."

I looked where she was pointing and saw a large blue bowl under the edge of the bed. *Gross.*

The idea of heading outside where the Three Stooges were probably still waiting for me was bad, but the thought of going to the bathroom in a bowl under my bed was even worse. So I headed downstairs. It turned out there was a back door to the hotel, and that a privy was actually a fancy word for an outhouse that smelled nearly as disgusting as a Scout camp port-a-potty.

CHAPTER 13

E xcept for a stack of dark blue overalls, the general store
didn't sell clothes. But the man behind the counter
pointed me to the shop of a tailor a few blocks down the
street. I kept watching for the guys from the woods, but they
must have given up waiting for me.

Mr. Finch, the tailor, was a skinny man with only a few
strands of hair combed across his mostly bald head.

He stuck a finger through the hole in my coat and shirt
with a frown. "How did this happen?"

I shrugged. "Moths?"

Apparently he didn't have any more sense of humor than
he did hair. Muttering something that sounded like, "What are
boys eating these days," he began running a tape measure up
my arms and around my chest. "You'll want to replace those
trousers as well?"

I wasn't sure how much this was going to cost, or even how

much money I had in my pocket. "Just the shirt and the coat, please."

He scowled and shook his head. But soon he had me dressed in a heavy, dark-green coat that came nearly to my knees and a tan shirt with a couple of buttons at the top and a weird kind of tie-string at the collar.

He glanced at my head. "You have a hat?"

"No, but that's—"

Before I could finish talking, he reached behind the counter and brought out a black hat with a rounded top. It reminded me of the one I'd seen Charlie Chaplin wearing in a silent movie our teacher showed us. I could just see myself walking around town with a black cane, slipping on banana peels.

Mr. Finch must have noticed me trying not to laugh, because he frowned and put the hat back under the counter.

"Do you have anything a little less fancy?" I asked.

He walked into the back of the store, muttering under his breath again. The only thing I caught was the word, "cheap." I grinned, wondering what he'd think if he knew I'd spent more than a hundred dollars for a pair of shoes just the week before.

"I assume you have something like *this* in mind," he said, dropping a hat onto the counter as if he could barely stand to touch it.

I picked up the hat and turned it over. It was dark brown and made of something that might have been felt. The top was still curved, but the brim was wide, and when I punched it down a little it looked kind of like something Indiana Jones would wear.

"Perfect. How much do I owe you?"

I handed over more of my money than I would have liked. I was pretty sure the guy was ripping me off, but since there weren't any price tags anywhere, what was I going to do?

Mr. Finch was starting to carry my old jacket and shirt into the back, when I remembered my letters. "Wait!" I shouted.

He grimaced as though I was asking to dig through his trash can as I pulled out the envelopes. I was tucking everything into my new coat when Ladan's second letter dropped to the floor.

As I picked it up, my gaze stopped on the last lines. *Your next message lies with the brother of the one you seek. Be Swift, time is running out.*

I hadn't noticed it before, but the word "swift" was capitalized. Was that a mistake, or did it mean something? It almost looked like it was a name. A clue?

"Excuse me," I said.

The tailor scowled. "You wish to paw through these filthy clothes again?"

"No. I was just wondering, is there anyone in town named Swift?"

He looked at me as if I was crazy. "Are you joking, boy?"

"No."

"Not from around here, are you?"

That was putting it mildly.

He set my old clothes down on the counter. "There are more Swifts in this town than you can shake a stick at. Palmyra Village was called Swift's Landing for years after the fellow who built the first grist mill. 'Course he's dead now. Couple of war heroes, too. Buried up at the Swift Cemetery. Now you want to talk about living, you've got . . ."

He began rattling off names of family members and where they lived, but by then I'd stopped listening. *Your message* lies *with the brother of the one you seek*. Not "the brother of the one you seek *has* your message." *Lies*. I hadn't realized how odd that word sounded until now. But it made sense if the brother was . . . dead.

I looked up from the letter. "The Swift Cemetery. Where is it?"

He crooked a finger. "Go to Church Street and walk a tenth of a mile toward the canal. It's up the hill on your left. You can't miss it."

◻   ◻   ◻

I could smell the canal before I reached it. It had a dank, musty smell. I could hear it, too. The sounds of animals and men. Chains clanking and wheels clunking across the planks of the bridge. Just as I reached it, I saw a pair of mules pulling a rope. At the end of the rope was a shallow, flat boat, painted a yellow and red so bright it looked like a carnival ride.

"Low bridge!" a voice bellowed. On the boat, all of the passengers ducked their heads to avoid hitting the bottom of the bridge.

"Out o' the way!" shouted a voice. I turned just in time to keep from being smashed by a wagon that came hurtling down the road behind me and over the bridge. Realizing I was standing in the middle of traffic, I stepped onto the shoulder.

I'd heard of the Erie Canal, but I'd never actually seen it. It was both more impressive than I'd expected, and less. For a canal that supposedly changed the entire face of shipping back in its day, it wasn't very big. Forty feet wide at the most, it narrowed quite a bit as it reached the water. From what I could see, it didn't look more than four or five feet deep. I was surprised boats could actually float on it.

But they did. Unlike Main Street, which had a kind of peaceful feeling to it, everything here seemed rough and fast. Men were shouting at one another, moving boxes and barrels on and off carts. Horses and oxen snorted and pulled at their harnesses. Men smoking huge cigars passed money back and forth.

I took a step back. I didn't want to be any closer to the canal than I had to be. I've got a thing about water. Maybe it comes from seeing *Jaws* on TV as a little kid, or maybe it's because I have all the buoyancy of a bowling ball. I don't swim, surf, paddle, or even wade if I can help it. The only thing I like to do with water is drink it.

But I could have stood around watching the bustling activity all day. I shook my head. I had a letter to find.

Just like the tailor had said, the cemetery was easy to locate. Several headstones were just visible on a hill overlooking the canal. As I climbed the grassy rise, more came into view. A rock wall ran along one side, with several large trees growing nearby.

I ran my fingers along several of the headstones. None of them looked very old.

General John Swift's, in the center of the graveyard, was the biggest. Beside it was a headstone for Elisha. Was that his brother? I searched around the tombstone, but couldn't see any sign of a letter. I continued along the lines of graves. Barnes. Harris. Hurlbut. Palmer. Robinson. Smith.

I nearly walked by the small stone marker, until I looked closer at the name. *Alvin Smith.* I wasn't a Church historian or anything, but I thought I remembered something about Joseph Smith having an older brother named Alvin. *The brother of the one you seek.* Was I seeking Joseph Smith? The idea of meeting him in person gave me goose bumps.

Kneeling on the ground, I began to search around the grave when a shadow passed over me.

"Ho there, what are you doing?"

I looked up into the eyes of a man staring angrily down at me.

"I, um . . ."

The man grabbed me by the arm and yanked me to my feet. He was strong. He stared at me with grim blue eyes. "What are you doing poking around my brother's grave?"

Was this the man I'd seen the night before? He looked similar, but not quite the same. I swallowed. "Are you . . . Joseph Smith?"

"I'm Hyrum." His eyes softened a little and his hand relaxed on my arm. "You know Joseph?"

How was I supposed to answer that? I'd heard of Joseph

Smith practically since I was old enough to walk. "Not personally. But I've heard a lot about him."

The man's eyes narrowed, but his expression was more of resignation than anger. "What have you heard?"

It was hard to believe I was actually standing beside the brother of the founder of the Church. What had I heard about Joseph Smith? What hadn't I heard? Sunday School lessons, Primary, seminary, firesides. I'd sung hymns written about his brother. I'd been to the jail where . . . where . . . All at once, my belly went cold. This was the man who, in the future, would stand by his brother's side and be shot to death by a mob.

But I couldn't say any of that. For one thing, he wouldn't believe me. And for another thing, I'd seen more than enough sci-fi movies to know you don't mess with the space-time continuum. Instead, I answered, "I'm not from around here, but I got a ride into town with Dr. Robinson. He had lots of good things to say about your family."

The corners of Hyrum's mouth rose into a relieved smile. "Sorry to come up on you like that. I thought . . ." He looked down at the headstone. "Joseph and I have always been the lighthearted ones in the family—playing games, pulling practical jokes. Alvin was more serious—a hard worker and very sober. Perhaps it comes from being the oldest. But lately, with all the persecution—all the things being said about my family—I find myself losing my sense of humor occasionally."

He released my arm and patted me on the shoulder. "I'm afraid there was talk a few years back of some scoundrels disturbing Alvin's body. I suppose that's why I reacted the way I did. I'm sorry."

I shrugged my shoulders. Hyrum was a little taller than Joseph, but not quite as wide through the shoulders. Still, I wouldn't want to be on his bad side. He had the look of a man who had spent a lot of time working with his arms and hands. "Not a problem, dude."

"Dude?" He tilted his head and smiled. His blue eyes gleamed. "You *aren't* from these parts, are you?"

"It's a long story," I said, still feeling a strange sense of unreality. "A friend sent me here. Well, I don't really know if you'd call him a friend. More like a teacher . . . or a tormenter even."

Hyrum laughed. "I think perhaps there's a little tormentor in all teachers."

He had a good laugh. I thought he would probably have made a pretty good football player too. "Anyway," I said, "I think he might have hidden a message for me somewhere around here. A letter."

"You mean like a game?" Hyrum immediately began scanning the grass and headstones. "There," he said, pointing to the low wall.

As soon as he pointed, I could see the envelope sticking out from between the stones. How could I have missed it? I grabbed the letter and shook it. The metal key piece inside made a small *shoosh-shoosh* sound against the paper.

"Hey, thanks," I said, tucking the envelope into my pocket.

"My pleasure." Hyrum glanced down the hill at the canal,

and his eyes got a distant look to them. "I like to come up here every now and then to visit with Alvin. He was serious, but like I said, he was a hard worker. I think the industry of the canal would have pleased him, even if the coarseness of the some of the workers wouldn't. Alvin had a certain nobility to him. I don't know if I'll ever have that."

I remembered the stories I'd heard of Hyrum standing by Joseph so many times. Remaining at his side in Carthage Jail, even when he knew it would probably mean his death. "I think you already have it."

He clapped me on the back. "I think you need to get your eyesight checked. But thank you all the same."

I needed to read the next letter, and get back to the hotel before the men from the woods came snooping around again, but I couldn't help asking something. "Your brother, Joseph . . . ?"

"Yes?" he asked.

"I know you're brothers and all . . ." I paused, trying to think how I would react if one of my younger brothers said he'd seen an angel. I think I'd probably give him a wedgie and tell him to quit making up stories.

Hyrum nodded as if he'd heard my thoughts. "So you *have* been in town long enough to hear stories about the Smith family."

I felt stupid. But I had to ask. "If my brother said he saw an angel, or spoke to God, I'd call him crazy. Do you believe Joseph really saw what he said he did?"

"I do," Hyrum said immediately. He seemed so sure.

"Joseph might be young—he's only twenty-one—but he doesn't lie. Of course, you can find out for yourself."

"You mean pray?" I asked, thinking of all the times my seminary teacher asked us to find out for ourselves if the Book of Mormon was true.

"Well, that's always a good idea," Hyrum said. His eyes twinkled. "But I was thinking about something a little more earthly. Like dinner."

At first I had no idea what he was talking about. How would dinner help me know if the Book of Mormon was true? Then I realized what he was saying. "Dinner with . . . with *Joseph Smith?*"

I must have sounded more than a little dumbstruck, because Hyrum roared with laughter. "Why not? He and Emma are in town for a few days. And Mother always loves to meet travelers. How does tomorrow night sound?"

"Sure. Okay," I mumbled, feeling numb all over.

I couldn't believe it. I was going to have dinner with the Prophet.

It had never occurred to me that being famous wasn't necessarily good. When I thought of fame, I thought of sports heroes or movie stars. Being famous lets them get into cool clubs and puts their faces on magazine covers. Even the guy who eats more hot dogs than anyone else gets sponsors and stuff. But what if you were famous for something like wrecking your new car the day after you got it? Or being the guy who dropped the pass that would have won the game? Or if everyone knew you as the kid who always smelled like cheese?

Suddenly fame didn't sound so good.

But even worse, what if the thing that made you famous also made everyone hate you? Because of something you said or something you did. If you knew you could make people stop hating you by saying you didn't really mean it, would you?

CHAPTER 14

I was so shocked by the idea of meeting Joseph Smith in person that I forgot all about the third letter until the next morning when I was downstairs having breakfast. When I did remember, I was amazed that I had waited all night before opening the envelope that would bring me one step closer to home. What did that say about me and what was going on? I pushed my plate aside and reached into my coat.

"Is everything to your liking?"

I looked up to see the man who had checked me into the hotel. Clasping his hands behind his back, he stared down at my plate.

"Yeah. It's great," I said, pushing my bacon around my plate with my fork. Somebody needed to tell these guys that bacon is supposed to be crisp. This stuff looked like they'd boiled it or something. "I'm just, uh, full."

He waved a hand, and the girl who'd told me about the bowl under my bed came and cleared my plate. I waited for the man to leave so I could read my letter in privacy, but he didn't seem to be in any hurry to go. He frowned down at me, and I wondered if he was waiting for a tip. "Is something wrong?"

"Are you a churchgoing man?" he asked.

With everything going on, I hadn't remembered today was Sunday. But now I got the guilty feeling in my stomach I always ended up with when I tried to convince my mom I was too sick to go to sacrament meeting. Then I realized the Mormon Church hadn't even been organized yet. How could I be blamed for not going?

I shifted in my chair. "I guess so. I mean, I do go to church." I didn't bother telling him I usually ended up cutting out early to get doughnuts with Jeff.

"Are you of the Presbyterian faith?"

"No."

Apparently my answer pleased him, because he gave me a brief smile, though it looked like his lips weren't used to pulling that far up. Then he frowned. "You're not a Baptist, are you?"

"Uh-uh," I said, and wondered what would have happened if I was.

That must have pleased him as well, because he patted me on the shoulder and gave me another of his pained smiles. "I knew it. A good Methodist."

Before I could decide whether or not to set him straight on that, he was pulling at my arm. "Let's get going. We don't want to be late for the service."

"I, uh, wasn't really planning on—" I started, but he clearly wasn't going to take no for an answer.

"I'm sure you'll like Pastor Wooster. If you haven't heard him before, he is a real fire-and-brimstone preacher. I haven't introduced myself. I'm Peter Westley."

Despite my arguments, Mr. Westley wouldn't let me get out of going with him. He was convinced that I was "in for a treat." I was convinced this was not a good idea. The next thing I knew, I was getting into his polished black carriage and sitting next to him and his wife, Elizabet.

I'd never been to a Methodist service before. In fact, except for my aunt's wedding, I'd never even been inside a non-LDS chapel. What if I didn't know the songs? What if they had ceremonies I was supposed to take part in? I could feel myself sweating inside my coat, even though the morning air was chilly.

The ride wasn't long, but the entire way, Mrs. Westley peppered me with questions about who I was, what I was doing here, and where I was from. I tried to avoid stepping into any major potholes as I danced around one question after another. Less than ten minutes after we left, we were pulling up in front of a small wooden building with a steep roof and long, narrow windows on each side of the door.

Mr. and Mrs. Westley each took one of my arms and walked me toward a tall man with long arms and legs. He wore a black suit and a white shirt that buttoned up to his neck.

"Pastor Wooster, I'd like you to meet a guest at my hotel— Kaleo Steele," Mr. Westley said.

"A pleasure to meet you," the pastor said, shaking my hand. "And where do you hail from?"

Sticking to the vague story I'd given the Westleys, I said, "I'm visiting from out west."

"I'd like to hear more about your travels," Pastor Wooster said.

Somehow I didn't think he would be nearly as enthusiastic if I told him about my *real* travels.

As the pastor turned to greet someone behind me, Mr. and Mrs. Westley walked me through the doors. The building was smaller than any chapel I'd ever been in before, with two rows of benches going up each side of the center aisle and a raised podium in the front. A woman in a frilly blue dress was playing the piano at the front of the building. Narrow windows with a kind of bubbly-looking glass filled the room with a dim light.

"I'll just sit in the back," I said, planning a quick getaway if things got out of hand.

"Nonsense," Mrs. Westley said. "You'll sit with us." Clutching my arm like she was afraid I'd turn and make a break for it—which I might have done if I'd been given the chance—she dragged me toward the front of the church and into the third row of pews on the left.

I was so busy trying to plan an escape that I didn't recognize the family sitting next to us on the bench until a familiar voice said, "Peter. Elizabet."

"Abel," Mr. Westley said. "How good to see you. Phoebe and Jennie, you two ladies look quite lovely."

Jennie? I spun around to find myself sitting only two spots away from the Jaggers.

"Allow me to introduce one of our guests at the hotel," Mr. Westley said.

Mr. Jagger scowled. "We've met."

Mrs. Westley turned from the Jaggers to me, sensing something was wrong.

"I didn't know you were a Methodist," Phoebe Jagger said to me, with a stare that was more than a little suspicious.

I scratched the back of my neck and tried to smile. "I guess we never got around to that."

"How did you meet Mr. Steele?" Peter Westley asked. "I thought he was new in town."

"He collapsed on my doorstep with a gunshot wound night before last," Mr. Jagger said, still with his lips pulled tightly down and his thick eyebrows bunched.

"Oh, my!" Elizabet's eyebrows rose, and I could tell she was wondering why I hadn't mentioned something like that on our ride over. She touched a hand softly to my shoulder. "Are you . . . all right?"

Mr. Jagger rolled his eyes. "Your guest is a quick healer."

All during the conversation, Jennie was watching me. I couldn't tell what she was thinking. She wasn't frowning at me like her mother and father, but she wasn't exactly smiling either. She looked, sort of, curious—the way you might study an albino alligator, or a rare species of monkey in a zoo.

I had just about decided to run for the exit and live with

the consequences, when Pastor Wooster walked to the pulpit and greeted the congregation.

Although the service was different from what I'd experienced in the past, I wasn't too lost. I closed my eyes during the prayer, and recognized some of the scriptures the pastor read out loud. When the collection plate was passed around, I dropped in a couple of coins.

Out of the corner of my eye, I could see Jennie watching me. She looked kind of cute with her honey-colored hair and red lips. But when I made the mistake of glancing in her direction, her father grimaced at me like a dog about to bite. I made sure not to look his way again.

After the congregation repeated the Lord's Prayer together, Pastor Wooster began his sermon. I'll be the first to admit, I don't do a real good job of paying attention in church. I tend to look around the room or flip through the hymn book. When I do pay attention to the speakers, I usually end up feeling guilty about something I should or shouldn't be doing, so I try to avoid it.

But Pastor Wooster didn't give me that choice. "There are sinners in our midst!" he boomed as soon as he stood up.

Instantly I felt my stomach tighten. I shot a quick look to my left and sure enough, Mr. Jagger was glaring at me like we both knew exactly who the preacher was talking about.

"Deceivers have come among us. Wolves in sheep's clothing."

Obviously the preacher knew I wasn't who I said I was. Had the Jaggers talked to him before the service? Or had Dr.

Robinson spread the word of how my bullet wound had magically healed? I could feel Jennie's eyes on me as my face heated up. The only question was whether I should duck my head and hope no one else knew who he was talking about, or run out the back door and make it clear. Would the Westleys even let me stay in their hotel after this?

Pastor Wooster flipped his Bible open and jammed a finger into the pages as though he was trying to run it straight through. "In the book of Revelation," he shouted, cords of muscle standing out on his neck, "St. John the Divine states, 'For I testify unto every man that heareth the words of the prophecy of this book, If any man shall add unto these things, God shall add unto him the plagues that are written in this book.'"

For a minute, I thought he was saying that I was going to be struck with some kind of Biblical plague. Then I recognized the scripture he was reading. It was one people sometimes use to argue how the Book of Mormon can't be true, because no scriptures can come after the book of Revelation. But Brother Mortensen had explained in seminary that the verse was only talking about the book of Revelation. Revelation wasn't even the last book in the Bible to be written. It was only put last when the books were gathered together.

But why would the preacher use that verse if he was talking about . . . ? Then it dawned on me. The preacher wasn't talking about me. He was talking about Joseph Smith. My first reaction was relief that I wasn't the subject of the preacher's scorn. I felt my cheeks cool a little, and when I peeked in Mr. Jagger's direction, he was no longer staring at me.

As I continued to listen to the preacher's sermon, I looked around at the rest of the people in the chapel. They were angry. Men and women glared up at the pulpit, saying things like, "Amen" and "You tell 'em."

"Brother and Sisters," Pastor Wooster shouted, pounding the pulpit, "some of the members of this village have taken to listening to the words of liars and scoundrels instead of clinging to the word of God. They have given heed to stories of angels and visions. They have gone in search of Bibles of gold. Listen to me now. Those who seek after such things—those who give ear to such stories—are damned! *Damned,* I say."

Walking through the tunnels, I'd thought that Joseph Smith wrote the Book of Mormon to get famous. He was famous here, all right. The more the preacher shouted, the angrier the people got, until they looked like they wanted to lynch Joseph—and maybe the whole Smith family while they were at it. And these were people who lived in the same town with him—people who'd known him and his family for ten years. How would people react who didn't know him? People who had only heard of him through the stories of angry ministers like this one?

For the first time, I began to really understand what it must have been like for Joseph. Had he known he would get this kind of response when he first told of seeing a vision? How could he have faced his neighbors, knowing the kinds of things they were saying about him?

The pastor was really worked up now. Sweat poured down his bright red face. "When Moses climbed the mount, God spake unto him and said, 'Thou canst not see my face: for there shall no man see me, and live!'" He slammed his Bible closed. "Can any man see God and live?"

"No!" the congregation shouted back.

"And if any man claims to have seen God, what is that man?"

"A liar!" Mr. and Mrs. Westley shouted together.

"And who is the father of lies?"

I glanced over at the Jaggers. Even Jennie was caught up in the excitement. "The devil," she called back, her blue eyes glowing with excitement.

I couldn't believe this. They were practically saying Joseph Smith and Satan were one and the same. Suddenly I remembered Ladan's words as we stood in his office together: *He is a liar and a cheat.* Is this what he sent me here to learn? Did he really believe Joseph Smith was a wicked man? I just couldn't see that. How could these people who seemed so ordinary—so nice—say these kinds of things about one of their own neighbors? A man who, as far as I could tell, had never harmed any of them?

My stomach felt sick. I wanted to walk out of the chapel and leave all the hatred behind. Instead I sunk down in my seat, trying to ignore the pastor's words, but unable to do so. All through the rest of the sermon, I couldn't help wondering what I'd do if I were in Joseph's shoes. Would I stand up to the ridicule, or would I back down from what I'd claimed?

Who was I kidding? I wasn't even brave enough to get up and leave the chapel. Instead I waited until the members were going to the front of the building to receive communion and snuck out the back door.

Dealing with a two-hundred-and-eighty pound linebacker is straightforward. He wants to shove your face in the turf, while causing as much pain as possible. You want to blow by him, with maybe a quick juke that leaves him looking silly, while you catch the ball on a fast crossing route.

Dealing with girls, on the other hand, is confusing to say the least. First off, they never tell you what they want. Does she like you? Does she like your friend? Does she like someone else entirely and wants him to see her with you so he'll get jealous?

Then there's the whole looks thing. A bad-tempered linebacker might look tough. He might curse you or try to jam a finger through your facemask. But that's nothing compared to when a girl opens her eyes, all wide and innocent, and drops her chin. She smiles just enough to form a dimple, then waits for you to melt. I've heard they actually practice this kind of thing in the mirror just to mess with you.

Give me a brush with death from a would-be killer on the football field over having to figure out a girl any day.

CHAPTER 15

The cool air felt great on my face as I stood outside the little chapel. Through the open door, I could hear the congregation singing. As I tried to decide whether I should wait for the Westleys or walk back to town on my own, I remembered the third letter. I still hadn't read it.

I walked to a grove of trees a few yards away from the chapel, and took the envelope from my pocket and opened it. Another tiny metal key piece dropped into my palm. I fitted it onto the metal rod, which was now starting to look like a real key.

My gaze dropped to the page.

"For as he thinketh in his heart, so is he . . ."

Kaleo,

By now I expect that you have had an opportunity to hear more than one opinion on the man who will come to be known by millions around the world as a latter-day prophet, and by millions more as a liar and a con man.

He definitely had that right, I could still hear the preacher's condemning words ringing in my ears.

The question you must answer for yourself is, what is in Joseph's heart? What would make him tell about the things he claimed to have seen, and never back down from it, even when his own life was the price to be paid?

I shook my head, realizing I didn't have an answer. Not fortune. I knew his family struggled financially their entire lives. And not fame. That question had been cleared up for me big time. Power, maybe? But for what purpose? An evil man would seek power to get his own way. But what did Joseph Smith use his power for? Maybe that's what I was supposed to figure out.

And lastly, you must decide what your own heart tells you. Your next message will be a major delivery.

Like all the other letters, it was signed,

From one witness to another,

Jadan

"It's cold out here." A girl's voice interrupted my reading, and I looked up from the letter to see Jennie pulling a light blue shawl around her shoulders. Quickly I shoved the letter and the key into my coat pocket.

"It feels like winter's almost here, doesn't it?" she asked. A bonnet was pulled low over her head, but her hands and face looked cold.

"Yeah," I mumbled, knowing I sounded like an idiot and trying not to notice how cute the tiny freckles looked on her pink cheeks.

She tilted her head, studying me, and I looked away from her eyes toward the church.

"Aren't you supposed to be back in there with the rest of them?" I asked.

"Do you want me to leave?"

This is why I hate talking to girls. They always end up putting words in your mouth. If I said I wanted her to leave, it would be rude. But if I said I didn't, she might take it as meaning I wanted to spend more time with her. Not that I had a problem with that or anything, it was just . . . complicated.

"I told my parents I wasn't feeling well," she said, when I didn't answer.

"I was feeling kind of sick too," I said. It was the truth. I just didn't tell her what I was feeling sick about.

"I feel fine." She tilted her head the other direction, dropping her chin almost to her chest and looking up at me through thick black eyelashes. "I just wanted to talk to you."

My heart started beating way too fast, and I had a strong urge to lick my lips that suddenly felt as dry as tree bark.

"A-about what?" Great, now I was stuttering. She had to think I was a total moron.

She folded her arms across her chest. "There's something different about you."

"You mean other than the fact that I sound like a complete idiot around girls?" The words spilled out of my mouth before I could stop them. And as soon as they left my lips, I wished I could take them back. Cool guys didn't admit they were embarrassed to talk to girls. But instead of being turned off, she threw back her head and laughed.

"Do you really?" she asked, her eyes twinkling with humor.

Why do girls always answer a question with questions of their own? "I was raised in a house of all brothers. I'm not real good at this kind of thing."

"What kind of thing is that?" She smirked, and I could tell she was teasing me.

I tried to shove my hands into my pants pockets, forgetting these pants didn't have any. Instead I balled my fists at my side. "The kind of thing where girls say stuff just to get you to put your foot in your mouth."

She bit her lip, trying not to laugh. "I'm sorry. It's just . . .

you don't seem like the sort of boy who would have problems talking to girls."

What was that supposed to mean?

Inside the church, the singing finished. Jennie glanced over her shoulder and looked back at me. "There *is* something different about you though."

"Different how?" The more we talked, the less uncomfortable I felt. She wasn't like most of the other girls I'd hung around with before, playing mind games and trying to get two guys to fight over them.

"For one thing, I've never met a boy who could heal from a gunshot wound overnight."

Here we go, I thought. *Try to get out of that one.* "Maybe it was a close miss."

"A close miss that gets blood all over your shirt, pants, and coat?" She shook her head, her blonde curls bobbing. "I don't think so. And it's not just that. You talk different, too. You wear your hair different. You even walk different. And when you were in our house, you kept looking around like you'd never seen anything like it before."

For a second, I considered telling her the truth. It would be nice to talk to someone openly and get everything off my chest. But I knew she'd think I was crazy. "I'm from out west," I said. The story had worked on the Westleys. But she narrowed her eyes.

"No. I've met frontiersmen before. Your hands aren't calloused. You don't look like you've spent that much time outdoors. I'll bet you can't even ride a horse."

She had me nailed. I was only surprised she was the first person to say it. "What do you want?"

She pressed her lips together with obvious satisfaction. "The truth. Who are you really?"

I laughed. "Trust me. You wouldn't believe the truth if I told you."

"Maybe you aren't giving me enough credit." She tapped the front of my coat. "What was that letter you were reading, and what was the thing you were holding that looked like a key?"

Suddenly I had to tell someone. If only to prove to myself that I wasn't going completely crazy. If she decided I was nuts, I'd live with it. But if she believed me . . . it would be so great to have someone to help me figure things out. I opened my mouth, but at that moment, people began coming out the door of the chapel.

Jennie spun around. "I have to go."

"Why?" I asked. "You asked me who I am. I—"

She raised a hand. "If people see me alone with a strange boy, they'll ask questions."

Did she just say I was *strange?*

She pulled her bonnet even further down over her eyes and looked away from me. "My father has a shop in town," she whispered. "Ask anyone where the Jagger blacksmith shop is, and they'll show you the way. Meet me around back tomorrow at ten."

"Okay."

She started to walk away, then glanced over her shoulder.

Her lips pulled up into a smirk, and she whispered quickly, "A boy as handsome and funny as you doesn't need to be shy around girls."

Then she was gone.

"There you are." Mr. Westley and his wife walked toward me across the grass.

"We wondered what happened to you," Mrs. Westley said.

"Stomachache," I answered, pretending to grimace.

"I hope it wasn't anything you ate." Mr. Westley's forehead wrinkled and his lips pulled down even more than normal.

"No." The last thing I wanted to do was offend them. "I just needed a little fresh air. I'm feeling much better now."

"We're having lunch with Pastor Wooster," Mrs. Westley said. "I told him you'd join us."

The thought of spending any more time with the man who'd ranted and raved about a person whose only crime was to say he'd seen an angel really did make me sick. Besides, Jennie had made it clear to me what a lousy liar I was. The farther away I stayed from nosy people, the better. "I don't think I'd better eat anything right now. I'll just walk back to town."

"Are you sure?" Mr. Westley asked. "A nice glass of wine might be just the thing to settle your stomach."

"Uh, no. But thanks for the offer."

Both Westleys looked a little ticked off. I wondered if bringing the new guy was how they'd managed to score lunch with the preacher. Before they could say anything though, I waved and started walking down the road. As I passed the church, I looked for Jennie. But she and her parents must have already left.

Probably for the best, I thought. *I don't think her mom liked me much, and I know her dad didn't.*

I'd walked about a mile down the road when I heard the clatter of hooves on the road behind me. I was getting pretty good at telling the difference between a carriage and a wagon, or a set of horses just by the sound. This one sounded like a wagon—probably pulled by a pair of horses. A dozen or so carriages and wagons had passed me, coming from the church and heading into town. I waited for this one to do the same, wanting to see if my guess was right.

Instead of passing, though, the horses slowed, then stopped. I started to look back—wondering if it was the Westleys, making one more try to bring me to lunch—when a man's voice called out.

"Well, lookie who we have here."

I spun around to see a man I knew all too well. Sitting next to him was a woman I didn't recognize, grinning nastily from the seat of the wagon. And climbing out of the back were his two buddies.

"Get 'im," Beer Belly growled.

I looked down the road. Now that the church traffic had passed by, there was no one in sight in either direction. Even with my improved vision I couldn't spot a single person nearby. I could outrun any of these clowns, but not the wagon. On the other side of the road was an open field. I didn't know if the wagon could get across that or not, but it definitely couldn't make it through the deep woods on my side.

"Gonna run?" Shorty asked, easing toward me.

I could lose them, but they'd just keep looking for me. Maybe it was the sneer on the little punk's face. Or maybe I was still feeling bad about not having the guts to walk out during Pastor Wooster's sermon. But I didn't feel like backing down anymore—even if it was three against one. I reached into a thicket of fallen branches near the side of the road and pulled out a stick about the length and thickness of a baseball bat.

"No," I said, slapping the branch against my open left palm. "I'm not going anywhere."

Long-tall-and-ugly ran his tongue over his lips and smiled. "You wanna fight, huh?"

He started toward me and I gauged his weight and speed. It wasn't that different from sizing up a defensive lineman. He had a couple of inches on me, but I was quicker. Plus, his balance looked a little off, like he might have been drinking—even though it was barely noon. I waited until he was almost within swinging distance, and then rammed the stick into his gut with both hands.

I was aiming for the spot just below his sternum. Put your helmet on a guy there and you knock the wind right out of him. I figured I'd go for one of his knees if that didn't work. But I didn't have to worry. As soon as I hit him, his face kind of puckered up, and he dropped to one knee. His mouth opened and closed like a fish flopping around on dry land.

I actually felt kind of sorry for him. Having the wind

knocked out of you is a scary feeling. But I didn't have time to waste. I still had the others to deal with.

Shorty gave a nervous laugh, exposing teeth that looked like they hadn't been brushed in years. "We still gotcha outnumbered."

Somehow I wasn't too worried. Having been raised in a house full of boys, and spending nearly every spare minute playing football with guys who were a lot bigger than I was, I'd learned how to stick up for myself.

"How many of your teeth do you think I could take out in one swing?" I asked, staring him down.

He blinked, his mouth snapping closed.

"Normally I'd say four or five, tops. But yours look kind of rotten. I'm thinking maybe a dozen if I hit it just right."

Beer Belly had been standing by the side of the wagon. Now he turned to the woman holding the reins and said, "Hand me my rifle. Let's see how that stick matches up against lead and powder."

"How'd that work for you last time?" I asked. In truth, if she had handed him the gun, I'd have been into the trees like a rabbit. Just because I seemed to heal miraculously fast didn't mean I wanted to take another chance with a bullet that might hit me in the heart or an artery. And I had no desire to find out if my healing extended all the way to rising from the dead.

My words seemed to do the trick though. Their leader turned away from the girl to stare at me.

"I shot you in the woods."

I stretched my arms and yawned just to show him I wasn't injured. "Do you see me in pain?"

"Maybe you missed?" Shorty asked.

Beer Belly's hand flashed out, and Shorty's head rocked backward. "I didn't miss. I saw him go down."

"I can take my shirt off and let you look for yourself if you'd like," I said, enjoying his confusion. "As long as it won't embarrass your girlfriend."

The woman in the wagon cackled, showing teeth that were just as brown as Shorty's. "Won't embarrass me none."

The big man frowned. "Who are you?"

One of the nice things about coming from the future is that you can use lines from movies no one has seen. I pulled my lip up, doing my best Sylvester Stallone sneer, and said, "I'm your worst nightmare."

The guy I'd jabbed in the gut finally managed to suck in a high-pitched, wheezing breath. "You're a friend of Joe Smith's," he said, holding his stomach.

"No, I'm not." I could tell none of them were sure how to take that. "Until I ran into him the night before last, I'd never met him."

Beer Belly shook his head, long blond hair flopping beneath the brim of his dirty hat. "If you wasn't no friend of his, what was you doing in the woods helping him?"

I didn't like any of these guys, but there was no reason to lie. "I'm new in town. I was lost in the woods when I ran into the three of you. Then he ran into me. What were *you* doing there?"

"Trying to get our share of the treasure," Shorty grunted.

"Shut up about the gold Bible," Beer Belly whispered. He meant it for Shorty's ears only, but with my improved hearing I had no problem listening in.

I couldn't help laughing. "You really believe in that?"

"What do you mean?" Long-tall-and-ugly asked as he got to his feet. His dark, piggy eyes studied me, and I could see he was thinking about trying another attack.

I shifted the stick in my hands. "You guys are such a bunch of dweebs. Do you really believe Joseph Smith saw an angel?"

Beer Belly snorted. "I don't believe a word comes out of Joe's lying mouth."

"Then why do you believe he actually has the gold plates?" I couldn't believe what total losers they were. "You don't believe anything he says, but you're out in the woods hunting for a 'gold Bible' you've never even seen. Hasn't it ever occurred to you he's making that up too?"

"He ain't making it up," the woman in the wagon said. She had wild, flyaway, brown hair, and a face that looked like she spent a lot of time outside.

"How do you know?" I asked.

She pulled something out of the folds of her dress. It gleamed green in the sun. "'Cause I seen it with my own eyes."

Shorty's lips rose into a dark smile. "How do you think we knew where to wait for him in the woods?"

I looked at the thing the woman was holding up. It looked like a piece of flat, polished rock. But the sun shone through it like green glass. "What is that?"

"It's my peep stone," she said. "I seen him through it."

"You saw him through your *rock?* Like a crystal ball or something?" I shook my head. What a load of superstitious garbage. "Well, that definitely makes it real for me then."

Beer Belly grabbed the guy I'd hit with the stick. "Show him."

Long-tall-and-ugly walked back to the wagon, hefted something out of the back, and dropped it in the road.

I didn't know what I was expecting. Another rock maybe? Certainly something more than the rotten log that hit the ground with an explosion of loose bark.

I looked at the tall man, wondering if I was supposed to be impressed. "If I watch it long enough, is it going to do something?"

Long-tall-and-ugly spat a brown string of chewing tobacco into the road. He leaned over, grabbed the log, and pulled back a long strip of bark. "What do you think'a that, smarty pants?"

At first I didn't know what he was talking about. Then I saw that part of the log had been carved away. Lighter wood stood out against the rotted log like someone had gone at it with a knife or a hatchet. The hollowed space was rectangular, maybe eight inches deep and nine or ten inches high by eight inches wide.

"Found it up on the side o' the hill where Smith claims the plates was buried," said Shorty. "That's where he hid 'em 'til night afore last."

"Still think the gold ain't real?" asked the woman, flashing her brown teeth.

Why would Joseph Smith go to all the trouble of carving a hole in a log to hide the plates if they weren't real? I couldn't imagine. Unless he was trying to convince these men that he had the plates. But why would he do that? "He showed this to you?"

"Joe didn't show us nothing," Beer Belly said. "He thinks he's too good to talk to the likes of us anymore. Sally found the hiding place with her peep stone. She found the hiding place. And she found the spot where we ambushed him. And she's going to find the gold, too. You might be a friend a' his and you might not, but you see him again, you tell him we aim to get our share one way or another."

The three men climbed back into the wagon. As they passed by, the leader called out, "We're gonna get that treasure. And anyone gets in our way will be sorry. That includes you."

It's funny how there are certain people that you don't really think of as people. Like when you run into your schoolteacher at the movies, and you're like, "Whoa, he's actually got a wife and kids. He has a real life outside the classroom." Or how you expect a movie star or a sports player to be just like they are on TV.

It's not that I thought of a prophet the same way I thought of a sports star. It's just that I always imagined Joseph Smith to be, I don't know, formal or something. Kind of stiff and reverent. I never thought of him as an actual person, not much older than I am.

Once again, I discovered I didn't have a clue.

CHAPTER 16

Later that afternoon, Hyrum stopped by the hotel to pick me up. Mr. and Mrs. Westley weren't around, but the guy behind the front desk gave both of us a glare as we headed for the hotel door.

"How do you stand it?" I asked Hyrum, and shot the desk clerk a dirty look of my own.

"What?" Hyrum glanced over his shoulder, following my gaze as we walked out the door. He laughed. "Oh, Kaleo. If I were to get upset over every scowl sent my way, I'd be fit to be tied all day and all night. I've learned it's easier to be a peacemaker than to argue with every ignorant soul who thinks badly of me."

We climbed onto the front seat of an old wooden wagon and he clucked the horses forward. As we started down Main Street, I thought about the things Pastor Wooster had said. "So you don't mind when people call Joseph a liar?"

Hyrum's jaws clenched, and I noticed his hands tighten

on the reins. "I didn't say that. People can say what they want about me. But when they attack my little brother, that's a different story. I'd defend Joseph to the death."

A chill ran down my back as I thought about how he would do just that in the Carthage Jail years from now.

Hyrum chuckled, lightening the mood. "A little dramatic I suppose. Sometimes the bitter words of people who should know better upset me. But I prefer to think of all the blessings our family has received instead of the persecution."

A light breeze picked up as the sun edged down toward the horizon and bits of hay blew around the back of the wagon. "What kinds of blessings?"

"The opportunity to witness God's church being restored to the earth in its fulness. Can you imagine any greater gift?" Hyrum smiled up at the sky with a dreamy look on his face. "After all the years of trying to get the plates—all the disappointment when Joseph came back from the hill empty-handed—I can hardly wait for him to begin translating. I stay up nights imagining what might be on them."

The plates. Again a chill raced down my spine. "Have you seen them?"

"Not yet. Joseph keeps them in a box for now. But he hopes that one day he will be able to show them to several people who can act as witnesses."

I remembered reading the testimony of the witnesses from the front of the Book of Mormon. I was pretty sure Hyrum was one of them. We rode for the next mile in silence.

"You look like you have something on your mind," Hyrum said.

In truth I'd been thinking about how excited Hyrum was about being able to read what was on the plates. I'd had the Book of Mormon in my house since I was born, and I'd never once taken the time to read it from cover to cover. I was too busy watching TV, or playing football, or anything else. But I couldn't tell him any of that. Instead, I said, "I went to the Methodist service with Mr. and Mrs. Westley today."

"Pastor Wooster," Hyrum said as we passed a large empty field.

I swallowed. "He said some things about Joseph."

I expected Hyrum to become upset, but he only nodded. "Pastor Wooster was one of the first people outside of the family Joseph told about his vision. Of all the sects in the area, the Methodists were the group Joseph was most partial to. He hoped the pastor would be as excited as he was at the news that God the Father and His Son Jesus Christ had returned to the earth."

Hyrum snorted a laugh and shook his head. "The pastor was not only unimpressed, but he told Joseph it all was of the devil. He said there were no such things as visions or revelations these days—that they had ceased with the Apostles. And that wasn't the end of it. You'd think the wealthy and powerful men would ignore the words of an obscure fourteen-year-old boy. But they ridiculed him and reviled him bitterly every chance they got. He didn't say much, but I know their treatment of him caused him a great deal of sorrow."

"How does he feel about them now?" I asked. "I could hardly stand listening to the sermon, and I wasn't even the one the pastor was talking about."

Hyrum slowed and turned from the dirt road into a driveway. Ahead I could see a two-story white house with green shutters. Smoke was billowing out of the chimney. "We're here," Hyrum said. "You can ask him for yourself."

□ □ □

The Smith family was just sitting down to dinner when we walked through the door. Mrs. Smith, a friendly-looking woman with dark hair that had started to turn gray, looked up as she set a basket of rolls onto a long wooden table covered with a blue cloth. "Oh, good, you made it. I was afraid we'd have to start without you."

"Which would have meant going hungry," said a woman with black hair pulled into a fancy bun on the back of her head. "With all the boys in this family, nothing set on the table lasts for long."

Being raised with a house full of brothers, I could relate.

As soon as she put the pot she was holding onto the center of the table, people came from everywhere, sliding onto the wooden benches on either side of the table. A boy, who looked to be ten or eleven, elbowed the girl next to him.

"Papa," said the girl who I guessed to be about fourteen, "tell Don Carlos to stop pushing."

"Katharine's trying to sit closest to the chicken and

dumplings," Don Carlos said, dropping his shoulder to get more leverage.

"Maybe we can help," said a boy who seemed to be about my age. He and another brother a few years older lifted the boy and girl and slid them to the end of the bench.

"Much better," said the older boy as he quickly climbed into the recently opened spot.

"No fair," hollered the younger boy and girl.

"Now, now," said a man who'd been reading near the fireplace. I assumed he was Hyrum's father. "Is this any way to treat our guest?"

"Better grab a spot, quick," Hyrum said.

He and I slid onto the bench, and the sound of a young girl's laughing scream was quickly followed by the sound of small feet clattering down the stairs.

"You'll never get away from me," called a deep voice.

The girl laughed again and came bounding down the stairs and into the living room. Just as she reached the large oval rug, a man leaped from staircase behind her. He landed on the floor with a thud and scooped her into his arms. "No one escapes Captain Rednose, the terror of the South Seas. Join my dastardly crew at once."

"No!" the girl shrieked, twisting and turning in his arms.

"Then I shall tickle you until you give in."

"You'll do no such thing," Mrs. Smith said, brandishing a long wooden spoon like a sword. "You'll both come and sit at this table before the food gets cold."

Hyrum leaned over and whispered, "That's Captain Rednose—also known as my brother Joseph."

Once everyone got settled at the table—sliding and squishing until we were all elbow to elbow—Mr. Smith bowed his head and clasped his hands together. Immediately all of the goofing around stopped, and everyone bowed their heads as Mr. Smith blessed the food.

After the blessing had been said, and the steaming chicken and dumplings had been served, Mrs. Smith smiled in my direction. "Hyrum tells us you are visiting from out west."

"It was sort of an unexpected trip," I said, quickly filling my mouth with food to keep from saying anything further.

"I want to go west," said the little girl.

"You want to go anywhere," Don Carlos said, shoveling food into his mouth so fast it was hard to believe he had time to swallow.

"Don't speak with your mouth full," said a woman who I guessed to be about Hyrum's age.

Mr. Smith laughed. "Little Lucy is our traveler. I wouldn't be surprised to see her journey all the way to the Pacific Ocean some day."

Though the meal was delicious, I could hardly taste it. I kept sneaking glances at the man sitting directly across from me. He was a little shorter than Hyrum, but he had the broad shoulders I remembered from the woods. I'd seen him in dozens of paintings and briefly in person a few nights before. Once or twice he met my gaze, and I quickly looked away from his piercing blue eyes.

Finally, the third or fourth time he caught me looking at him, he grinned. "Our guest has a powerful shoulder."

The woman sitting by his side with the dark hair—I guessed she must be his wife, Emma—looked across the table at me. "You two have met?"

I wasn't sure how to answer that. Did he want people to know how we'd bumped into each other?

Fortunately Joseph spoke up. "The night before last, when I was coming back with the plates, I ran into a little trouble."

"Samuel Lawrence and Alva Beaman," said the boy who looked about my age.

Joseph nodded. "It might have been, William. I couldn't tell for sure in the dark. There were three of them. Fortunately our guest showed up at just the right time. He put a lick on one of them so hard I was afraid it would knock the trees over right on top of me."

Lucy giggled.

"I owe you my thanks," Joseph said to me.

I shrugged, feeling everyone's eyes on me. "You helped me as much as I helped you. The fat one was just about to put the butt of his rifle through my head when you stopped him."

Joseph rubbed his thumb, which was still purple and swollen. He took another roll and began to butter it while still watching me. "What were you doing in the woods?"

"I was actually a little lost at the time," I said. Joseph studied me as though waiting for more. I could feel cold sweat run down my back. If this conversation went too far, I could get into trouble.

Hyrum tapped me on the elbow. "Quick—grab me one of those rolls before Joseph eats them all."

Joseph rolled his eyes comically. "Here," he said with a grin. "You can take mine." With a flick of his wrist, he flung his roll across the table, hitting Hyrum in the face with it.

"This is war," Hyrum growled. He was reaching for a roll to throw himself when Mrs. Smith smacked him on the back of the hand with her wooden spoon.

"There'll be none of that at my table."

Emma shook her head as the younger Smith children laughed. "Just because you've broken a horse doesn't mean it's trained."

"What makes you think I'm broken?" Joseph asked, putting his arm around his wife. As everyone finished the last of their dinner, he smiled and patted his stomach. "That was a delicious dinner, Mother. After nourishing our bodies, perhaps we can nourish our minds?"

Mr. Smith nodded. "I think that's a fine idea. Let's carry the benches in by the fire."

With so many hands helping, the table was quickly cleared, and everyone gathered in the living room.

"Kaleo has a question for you," Hyrum said to Joseph, setting another log into the fireplace.

"Do you?" Joseph looked at me again with eyes that seemed to see deeper than they possibly could. "Anything for the man who came to my aid in my time of need." He folded his arms across his chest, and my mouth went dry.

I tried to speak, but the only thing that came out was a

froglike croak. Don Carlos and Katharine chuckled, and their mother scowled at them.

Sensing my embarrassment, Hyrum saved me again. "Kaleo attended the Methodist services today. Pastor Wooster was in fine form."

"That man . . ." Mrs. Smith frowned, the lines in her forehead bunching. But Joseph held up a hand.

"Now, Mother, let's not speak ill of others." He looked at me. "I assume he had something to say about me?"

I licked my lips. "How can you stand it? If people were talking that way about me I'd probably end up punching somebody in the mouth."

"I'd help you," Lucy squeaked, bunching her tiny fist. No one in the room could help laughing.

Joseph called the youngest Smith child over and plopped her onto his lap. He looked into the crackling flames. "The biggest difference between me and the other faiths is that they are limited in what they can accept by their individual creeds." He touched his forefingers and thumbs together to form a circle. "Their creeds set up stakes that say, 'Hitherto shalt thou come and no further.' This deprives their members of believing anything not contained in their creed. I am ready to believe all true principles that exist as they are made manifest."

I shook my head. "But when they say those things about you . . ."

Joseph patted Lucy. "When men open their lips against the truth, they do not injure me, but themselves."

"They're all convinced revelation has ended," Mrs. Smith said.

Joseph sighed. "They preach of being saved. But man is saved no faster than he gains knowledge."

The heat of the fire had started to lull me to sleep, but at the word knowledge I perked up. *Knowledge is the key,* the letter had said.

"Knowledge does away with darkness, suspense and doubt; for these cannot exist where knowledge is." Joseph leaned forward, his eyes shining. He didn't look any different than he had at the table, but as he spoke there was something in his voice that made him seem older. "In knowledge there is power. God has more power than all the other beings, because He has greater knowledge."

Listening to Joseph, I felt something I hadn't felt with all the rantings and ravings of Pastor Wooster. I felt . . . truth. I knew that what Joseph was saying was important to my getting back home, but I still wasn't sure how.

Joseph turned and looked straight at me, almost as if I'd asked him the question in my mind. "If man does not get knowledge he will be brought into captivity by some evil power of the other world, as evil spirits have more knowledge, and consequently more power than many men who are on the Earth."

Mr. Smith opened his mouth as if he was about to say something, but at that moment, Joseph's eyes went wide. He set Lucy on the floor and leaped to his feet.

Emma stood up as well, watching her husband anxiously. "Joseph, what is it?"

Joseph tilted his head as if listening to something no one else could hear. I strained to catch any sound, but even with my enhanced senses, I couldn't make out anything except for the breathing of the people around me and the popping and snapping of the logs being consumed by the fire.

Without a word, Joseph raced up the stairs.

"The plates," Emma whispered, her voice barely audible.

Hyrum ran to the door. He cracked it open and looked out.

"Do you see anything?" his father asked.

"No." Hyrum closed the door and blocked it with a heavy beam.

A moment later, Joseph came running down the stairs. He held a rectangular box clutched to his chest. Goose bumps rose on my arms and back. "Father, lift the loose stone on the hearth."

"What is it?" Mrs. Smith asked. "What's wrong?"

Mr. Smith tugged a long flat stone away from the front of the fireplace. Joseph set the box inside the opening, and he and his father together slid the stone back in place. "They're coming for the plates," Joseph said, his eyes searching the room. "They'll be here any minute."

"How can you be sure?" Don Carlos asked.

Before Joseph could answer, I heard something outside. "Voices," I said, my heart racing. "It sounds like a lot of them."

"If we stay quiet, maybe they'll go away," Joseph's older sister Sophronia said.

"No." Joseph glanced toward the door. "Their numbers are greater this time. Their confidence will only grow if we back down."

As if to back up his claim, a voice shouted. "Bring out them plates, Smith! They're ours as much as yours."

"Then we fight," Sam said, clenching his fists.

Hyrum moved to stand by his brother's side, his eyes steel. Mr. Smith joined the two of them along with Sam and Don Carlos.

Someone fired a gun outside, and what sounded like a rock slammed against one of the walls. "Come out or we'll come in and get you!" yelled a man's voice.

Joseph looked at me, and for a second I could swear my heart actually stopped. "They have guns this time," he said. "You put your life on the line for me once. I can't ask you to do it again."

I tried to swallow and couldn't. I looked toward the hearth where the box was hidden. I wanted to tell him, "Just open it and tell everyone you made the whole thing up." But what if he hadn't made it up? What if there really were gold plates in there?

I wasn't sure my legs would hold me. Somehow though, I ended up standing beside the five Smith brothers.

Hyrum slapped me on the shoulder and turned to Joseph. "What do you want us to do, brother?"

Slowly a smile crept across Joseph's face. "We don't know how many of them are outside. But they don't know how many of us are in here."

He gathered everyone together and told us his plan. I couldn't believe what I was hearing. There were men with guns outside—men who weren't afraid to use them to get their share of what they considered an invaluable treasure. Joseph's idea was the craziest thing I'd ever heard, yet the rest of the family bought into it at once.

Each of the men walked to the fireplace and grabbed a stick of wood, while the women gathered pots and pans.

"When I count three," Joseph whispered.

I gripped my log with sweaty palms, wondering if I was about to die.

"One . . . two . . ."

Hyrum grabbed the door, and we all got ready to run.

"Three." On Joseph's count, Hyrum threw open the door with a loud whoop. Behind him, all the Smith women began banging their pots and pans. Holding my stick of wood high in the air, I waved it back and forth and shouted at the top of my lungs. To my right and left, the Smith brothers were doing the same thing. It sounded like a pack of orangutans had broken out of their cages and were trying to take over the zoo.

As we raced out the door, I could make out half a dozen or so men, standing just out of the light of the doorway. At our appearance, one of the men raised his rifle and fired wildly into the air, and for a second I thought they were going to attack.

"Yee haw!" Joseph yelled, racing by me on the left.

"Get 'em!" Father Smith hollered. He looked like he was having the time of his life.

I don't know whether it was our shouting, along with the banging of the pans, or the sudden appearance of so many people racing out of the house, but as we ran forward, one of the men turned in retreat. "Fall back!" he yelled.

Another man broke and ran.

Before we'd gotten to within twenty feet of them, all of the men were racing away as if a pack of wolves was hot on their heels.

"Look at them go!" Hyrum yelled.

"Cowards!" Don Carlos shouted, waving his log like a sword.

With my pulse pounding in my chest, I stood watching the group of men disappear into the trees across the road. We'd done it. We'd actually scared off a crowd of armed men with nothing more than sticks and pans.

I started to turn back to the house, when I realized someone was standing only a few feet away. I thought at first it was one of the Smiths. But as the ghostly figure glided from the shadows of a tall hickory tree into the moonlight, I knew I'd never seen him before. Though he was a little shorter than I was, his bony limbs and gaunt face made him appear taller. Clumps of dark hair poked up wildly from the sides and top of his head. His pale-white skin glowed like a spirit under the moon, and a beard hung nearly to his chest. I was sure it had to be a trick of the light, but it looked like half of his beard was white, while the other half was jet-black.

The figure stepped straight toward me. As he drew close, his eyes seemed to blaze with their own inner fire, and I could see that something was wrong with his face. Three snakelike scars curved up the side of his right cheek, as though something had ripped at him with its claws.

I stumbled backward, almost believing I had imagined him. But he was real enough. He raised a hand, and the sleeve of his dark jacket flapped in a cold breeze that came out of nowhere.

He pointed a gnarled finger at me and whispered, "You have been marked, boy." Then he disappeared into the darkness.

I woke up Monday morning thinking what a weird night it had been. Eating with Joseph Smith, scaring off armed men with a bunch of logs, meeting a guy who seemed more ghost than human. I thought it had probably been the weirdest day of my life. I had no idea things were going to get much, much weirder.

CHAPTER 17

My head was still spinning the next morning—as much from meeting Joseph Smith as from the attack afterward. I honestly didn't know what to think. When I pictured a prophet, I imagined a man in a dark suit speaking in general conference. Or maybe an old guy in a white robe with a long beard preaching from a mountain-top. Joseph Smith was only a few years older than I was. He cracked jokes. He threw food.

Did prophets do that?

I didn't know if President Hinckley had ever thrown food, but I *had* heard him tell a joke or two in conference. And President Monson often told funny stories. But still, meeting the actual Joseph Smith—not an actor playing him—and see-ing he was a normal person made it that much harder to imag-ine him seeing Heavenly Father and Jesus face-to-face.

Somehow he'd known the people were coming for the plates before they ever showed up. Could he have done that if he wasn't a prophet? And then there were the plates themselves. Of course I hadn't seen what was inside the box. For all I knew it could have been a bunch of rocks.

Except why go to all the trouble of hiding a box if there were only rocks in it? If I were pretending to have gold plates, I wouldn't show them at all. I'd have told everyone they were hidden somewhere they'd never find them. Keeping a box around just gave that much more encouragement to the people who were determined to get them.

And now those same people thought I was helping Joseph. None of the Smiths had seen the creepy dude in the woods, but I knew he'd been real, and the words he'd spoken still gave me chills. I didn't know what he meant by, "You have been marked," but it couldn't be anything good. I needed to get the rest of the key and get back home before things got worse.

Unfortunately, I had no idea where the next letter was. The only clue I had was that it would be a *major delivery,* whatever that meant

I glanced at the big grandfather clock in the hotel lobby. It was nine-thirty. That gave me half an hour before I was supposed to meet Jennie. Maybe I could use the time to figure out where the next letter was.

"Kaleo." I turned to see Mr. Westley watching me from behind the hotel check-in desk. He looked even grumpier than usual.

"We missed you at dinner last night," he said, brushing something from the sleeve of his jacket.

"Yeah. Sorry about that. I was with . . ." I started to say

"the Smiths" before remembering the pastor's sermon from the day before. Something told me bringing up the Smith name might not be the best idea. "I was having dinner with someone else."

"So I understand." The look in his eyes told me he knew exactly where I'd been anyway. He coughed a little *hem-hem* into his fist. "Far be it from me to tell any of my guests whom to consort with."

"But you're going to anyway?" I said, unable to help myself. The guy was really getting on my nerves.

His eyes flashed. "The Smiths are not the sort of people you should be spending time with."

I could tell from his tone of voice that I was going to find myself out on the street if I wasn't careful. But I'd had enough of listening to false accusations. "Has Joseph Smith or any of his family ever done anything to you?" I asked.

He glared, his lips pressing together until they were nearly white.

"Have they done anything to Pastor Wooster?"

"I hardly think that's—"

My parents had taught me to never intentionally interrupt an adult before, but I'd had it. "I'm only asking because I've seen stray dogs treated better than a lot of you seem to treat the Smith family. I've seen them attacked physically and with words. I've heard them called liars, cheats, and followers of Satan. Yes, I had dinner with them last night. And you know what? Joseph and his family didn't have one bad thing to say about you or the pastor. He was hurt that so many people treat him and his family badly. But he didn't attack your character. So tell me, what has he done to you personally that makes you hate him so much?"

He held out his hands, as if I'd threatened to attack him, and scowled. "Mark my words, young man. Joe Smith is a snake. People who sleep with snakes get bitten sooner or later."

I'd heard enough of his kind of talk. I pushed open the door. Before I walked out though, I looked over my shoulder. "Maybe you should look in the mirror and see who really has fangs."

Way to keep your temper under control, I thought as I headed down the street. At this rate, I'd have the entire town hating me before the week was out.

I stopped a man in an expensive-looking gray and black suit. "Excuse me," I said. "Could you tell me where I could find Mr. Jagger, the blacksmith?"

He pointed in the direction he'd been walking. "A block and a half down on the right."

"Thanks." As he started away, an idea occurred to me. "Is there a post office or something around here?"

"Postmaster's office is just up the street," he said, gesturing toward a small wooden building. "Major Obadiah Dickerson is the man you're looking for."

Major Dickerson. A *major* delivery. That had to be it. "Thanks again," I said, breaking into a jog.

"Of course, you won't find him there," the man called.

I stopped and wheeled around. "Why not?"

"He's never in his office. Spends most of his time hunting, fishing, or wandering around town."

"But what about the letters?" I asked, wondering what kind of postman spent his days out hunting and fishing.

The man grinned and tapped his head. "Obadiah keeps all of his important papers and letters in the lining of his big bell-crown hat. If you're expecting something, your best bet is to ask around town. Someone is sure to have seen him. Or wait long enough and he'll find you."

Great. Just what I needed. A postman who kept all his letters in his hat. I could imagine Ladan laughing at my frustration.

Since the post office was out, I headed to Mr. Jagger's shop instead. Jennie was right, the blacksmith shop was easy to find. The sound of metal hammering against metal rang through the air, long before I reached the building. Above the wide doorway, *Jagger* was spelled out in intricate iron letters.

The interior of the shop was dark, but I could hear the constant *clank-clank, clank-clank* of hammering coming from inside, and the air smelled of fire and metal.

A long, slow whistle sounded from the side of the building. I looked around before spotting Jennie waving me toward the back. I followed her down a narrow alley between the blacksmith and a bakery that had incredible smells drifting out of its chimney.

"Come with me," Jennie said, grabbing my arm and pulling me around the back of the building. "If my father sees you, we won't be able to talk."

"He doesn't like me much," I said as she led me through a maze of empty boxes and barrels.

"He thinks you practice black magic." We stopped beneath the branches of a large oak tree that had lost most of its leaves. She stared at me from beneath the brim of a dark green bonnet. "Do you?"

"Do I what?"

"Practice dark magic."

I thought she was joking and couldn't help laughing. She stared at me in stony silence. I'd noticed before that her eyes were blue, but now the bonnet she was wearing brought out tiny flecks of green. "You're kidding, right?"

She reached up and tugged at a honey-colored strand of her hair, fuming. "It's not funny. There's something strange about you, and I demand to know what it is."

I'd had girls accuse me of a lot of things in the past. Usually they thought I was full of myself because I was quiet, or they figured I was a "dumb jock." But I'd never been accused of being a magician. I swallowed, trying to get my laughter under control. "No," I said, when I thought I could keep a straight face. "I do not practice dark magic. I don't practice any kind of magic. I even stink at card tricks."

She poked the shoulder where I'd been shot. "Then how do you explain that?"

Something fell over in the stacks of boxes, and I spun around.

"It's just one of the cats," she said. "They keep away the rats that are drawn by the smell of fresh-baked bread."

When nothing else moved, I studied her for a minute, wondering how far I could trust her. "What if I told you I'm not from here?"

She sniffed. "I've figured that much out."

I considered my options. She already thought I was some kind of evil wizard. What could be worse? "Okay. So you know I'm not from here. The thing is . . . ." I tried to think of how to put it. "I'm from a lot farther away than you would probably believe. And I didn't get here by boat, or by coach, or by horseback. I made a mistake, and this man . . . sent me into some tunnels to teach me a lesson. The tunnels brought me out here."

"This man was one of the nee-fights my father hired?"

"Nephites," I said, correcting her pronunciation. "I think so."

She seemed to be taking it much better than I expected. "Are these Nephites wizards of some kind?"

That was a great question. I wished I had a great answer. "I'm pretty sure not. And they definitely don't practice dark magic. In fact, I think they sent me here to sort out my feelings about Heavenly Father and Jesus."

She peeled a piece of bark from the tree, and I could see her trying to decide whether or not she believed me. "Why don't you just go back?"

"I wish I could," I sighed. "But it's not that easy." I reached into my pocket and pulled out the black rod. "The door that leads into the tunnels I came through is locked, and I can't get through it without the key. But this is only part of it. The other pieces of the key are in letters, and I can't open the door until I get them all."

Something flashed in her eyes as I showed her the rod.

"Surely you could find your way back without entering the tunnels," she said. "Even if it is a long distance."

I shook my head. "The only way to get there is through the door."

Her fingers stroked a thin silver chain that hung from her neck and disappeared down the front of her dress. I could tell she still wasn't sure if she believed me, so I took a piece of bark from her fingers. "Watch," I said, lightly scraping the bark across the inside of my arm. The wood left a thin, red mark. "You asked me how I healed from the gunshot."

For a moment nothing happened. She looked up from my arm and as her eyes met mine, I could feel my face heating up. "Keep watching," I said.

Then it happened. One second the scratch was there, my skin rough and ragged red. The next second it was gone—replaced by pink new skin.

Her eyes went wide and her fingers clamped closed around the necklace as she stepped back. "You *are* a wizard!"

"It's not magic," I said. "At least not the way *I* think of magic. But I'm pretty sure it's got something to do with how I got here. Ever since I came through the door, any injury I get heals. I can hear better and see a lot farther, too."

I could tell she was about to run away, and suddenly I didn't want her to. I had to have someone believe me, if only to convince myself I wasn't totally crazy. "You know I'm not from this place. But the thing is, I'm not from this time either. I live a long time in the future. At least I did until my seminary teacher caught me holding a beer with some guys from my football team." Words poured from my mouth before I could think about whether saying them was a bad idea.

"See, I didn't believe Joseph Smith really found the gold plates or saw an angel. I got sent to meet this guy named Ladan. I guess he figured I'd never believe him unless I saw for myself. He put me in these old clothes and, I have no idea how he did it, but somehow he sent me clear across the country and back in time almost two hundred years."

"Two . . . hundred . . . years." The words slipped from between her lips one at a time. Her eyes were opened so wide it looked like her eyeballs would roll out onto the ground any second.

"You think I made it all up."

Jennie put her hands to her mouth. I expected her to be scared, skeptical—maybe even upset. What I didn't expect were the giggles that forced their way through her fingers. She was laughing—at *me*. Giggles turned to outright guffaws. She laughed so hard she was shaking. Tears poured from her eyes and she rocked back and forth on the balls of her feet.

"Fine. Just forget it." I felt my face go red. Not with embarrassment this time, but anger.

It had been a stupid idea to tell a stupid girl something that was stupid anyway. "I don't care if you don't believe me," I said. "I've got better things to do anyway."

I started to walk away, but she grabbed me by the arm.

Still laughing, she shook her head. "No," she managed between snorts. "I—" She tried to speak, but burst into howls of laughter again. She clapped her hands to her stomach and blurted, "I do. I believe you."

"You *do*?" I asked, pretty sure she was messing with me.

"Yes," she said, wiping her hands across her eyes.

"Why?" I was upset when I thought she didn't believe me. Now it was hard to imagine how she possibly could. If someone came to Copper Hills High and told me they were from the future, I'd have called him a liar for sure.

Jennie took a deep breath. A few minutes earlier, I'd been trying to get my own laughter under control. Now it was my turn to wait impatiently while she tried to keep from giggling. "It's the only thing that makes sense," she said with a grin.

I ran my fingers through my hair. "What's that supposed to mean?"

"I knew there was something odd about you from the first moment you collapsed in my front yard."

"You're calling me odd?" This was not the way I expected this conversation to go. She was supposed to think I was an awesome time traveler. Not *odd*. She bit her lower lip, and I could tell she was trying not to start laughing again. I had to admit she really was cute with her upturned nose and freckled cheeks. But *odd*?

"Not in a bad way. You're unlike any boy I've ever met. Your accent, the words you use—words I've never heard of—the things that surprise you, and the things you seem to take for granted. At first I thought you were from some big city, looking down your nose at us country folks. I didn't want to like you—especially after what my father said about you. But I couldn't help myself."

"You couldn't? I mean, you don't? Dislike me, that is. You *do* like me?" My tongue seemed incapable of putting even the most basic words together into a sentence that made sense. But she didn't seem to mind.

"Yes." She nodded, her gaze dropping. "Does that surprise you?"

"No. Well, yes."

She laughed, and for once I didn't mind. "Ever since I met you I've been trying to understand what it was about you. You didn't sound foreign, but you didn't sound like you were from America either. I couldn't believe you practiced magic, but so many things you did were inexplicable." Her eyes bored into mine. "What's it like? In the future?"

I opened my mouth, then closed it, unsure of what to say. "In some ways it's great. Better medicine. Faster travel. You'd be amazed if I told you about cell phones. But in other ways . . ." I looked up at the clear blue sky without a trace of smog, and smelled the air. "In other ways, this is pretty great too."

Jennie looked down and chewed on the tip of her thumb. "Would you ever consider . . . staying?"

Before I could answer, something clanged to the ground nearby.

"It's my father," Jennie hissed. "Quick—you have to get out of here."

"Maybe I could talk to him," I suggested. "Explain that I don't do magic."

"No." She shook her head and her hand went to her necklace again. "You have to go."

She pushed me toward the alley on the side of the black-smith shop, then grabbed my arm and pulled me back. "This afternoon," she said, her face pale and her eyes serious. "Come to my house. I have something I need to tell you."

I watched her disappear through the stacks and barrels before I turned and started up the alley. I hadn't gone more than a few steps when I heard something behind me. I spun around just in time to see a long metal rod swing through the air and hit me dead center on my forehead.

In the movies, the hero who gets hit over the head always slumps to the floor, unconscious, while the bad guy steals the secret plans. In my experience, that almost never happens. They call it "getting your bell rung" in football, and that's probably a pretty good comparison. Getting a direct hit to the head—even when you're wearing a helmet—is like being inside a giant bell. It shakes you all the way from your head to your toes. Sometimes you hear a ringing in your ears, sometimes not, but you always feel like you just got nailed by a truck.

You think you're okay until you try to get up and walk. That's when you realize all the circuits in your brain got temporarily scrambled. Your feet won't go where you want them to. Your eyes have a hard time focusing. And even the easiest questions seem like complex math algorithms.

Maybe the spies and private investigators in movies know exactly where to hit a guy to make him drop like a sack of rocks—or maybe it's the difference of wearing a helmet—but I think it's more likely that the movie directors don't want a bunch of bad guys wandering around going, "Wait, where am I again, Coach?"

CHAPTER 18

I tried to pull away from the men who picked me up and dragged me though the woods, but all I managed was a feeble moan.

"Get him out of here," said a voice I recognized. I rolled my eyes up to see Jennie's father holding a long piece of metal.

"Tie his hands and legs," somebody else said, and I felt my wrists yanked backwards as a length of rope bit into my skin. Several pairs of hands lifted me up and threw me into the back of a wagon.

"Not feeling so tough now, are you?" Crouched in the back of the wagon, Shorty shoved his face only inches from mine. I could smell alcohol and chewing tobacco on his breath. I tried to spit at him, but couldn't draw any saliva into my mouth. He grinned and slugged me in the stomach.

"Watch it back there," a voice said. "Blackburn wants him in one piece."

Shorty launched a wad of tobacco spit over the side of the

wagon and gave a wet-sounding chuckle. Even in my woozy state, it was a chilling sound. "Probably wants to cut him up piece by piece himself."

The wagon jerked forward, rattling me against the floor-boards. As the wheels rumbled across the rough dirt road, shaking me around like I was riding the world's roughest roller-coaster, I tried to pull my thoughts together, but it was hard to think.

Why had Jennie's father hit me? Was he working to get the plates too, or was he just trying to get rid of me? Jennie couldn't have known about what her father was up to, but she was obviously scared of him discovering me. And somehow he had known I was there.

My neck felt like it had bolts sticking into each side—like the monster in *Frankenstein*—and it nearly killed me to turn my head enough to make out Shorty and Long-tall-and-ugly squatting in the back of the wagon watching me.

"Enjoying the ride?" The tall goon giggled, baring his few teeth and tobacco-stained tongue.

"Where are you taking me?" I mumbled. Talking hurt almost as much as turning my head did.

Shorty spat over the side of the wagon again. "Think we should tell him?"

"Why not?" his companion said, shrugging his skinny shoulders.

I wanted to punch their sneering faces and knock them out of the back of the wagon. But I could barely move.

"Ever hear tell of Alistair Blackburn?" Shorty asked,

holding the side boards and sitting on the heels of his boots to keep off the splintery boards of the bouncing wagon.

I shook my head and immediately regretted it as jolts of pain shot up my neck.

"He's heard of *you*," laughed a female voice from the front of the wagon. In my current position I couldn't see who was talking, but I was pretty sure it was the girl I'd seen with these head-cases when they'd stopped me the day before. I think someone had called her Sally.

"How could he?" I asked. "I just got into town a couple of days ago."

"Mr. Blackburn knows lots of things—things you wouldn't believe." Long-tall-and-ugly's eyes went so wide it would have been comical if his voice hadn't been so serious. It took me a minute to realize he was afraid of whoever this Blackburn guy was. "He knows things that happened a long time ago—before there was writing and such—and things that ain't happened yet. He knows where things is and where things is gonna be."

"He knows how to read the stars and talk to the spirits." Shorty nodded solemnly. The guy sounded like a fortune-teller to me—the kind of person who charges twenty bucks to read your horoscope or mumble nonsense over a crystal ball—but he obviously had these two convinced.

"What does he want with me?" My head was starting to ache a little less, but my neck still felt like it was on fire.

Shorty licked his lips. "He knows all about you. He says you been hiding a secret."

My secret? He couldn't possibly know that. Still, I felt a cold fist of ice form in the pit of my stomach.

Long-tall-and ugly sneered at me, his eyes black even in the bright morning light. "He says he's got a job for you."

"That's enough talking," called a voice I recognized as the leader of this cheerful little group. "He wants to know about Blackburn, he can talk to him hisself. Now everybody stop flapping your lips 'til we get there."

I couldn't get anyone to respond to any more of my questions and finally gave up asking. For the rest of the ride, Shorty and his friend watched me as if they were a studying a pig about to be slaughtered.

Ten or fifteen minutes later, the wagon jerked to a stop. I hadn't been able to see anything but sky and an occasional tree branch as I lay on the bottom of the bouncing wagon, but as the two men yanked me to my feet, I saw we were parked in front of a small wooden cabin. Several other horses and wagons were parked nearby, and behind the cabin, I could see the greenish water of a pond.

"On your feet," Shorty called as they dropped me over the side. My head was feeling screwed on a little tighter, and I was prepared to make a break for it as soon as my feet touched the ground. What I hadn't counted on was my feet having fallen asleep during the ride. My legs collapsed out from under me, and, with my hands still tied behind my back, I fell face-first, getting a mouthful of dirt.

"Oops." The leader laughed—his gut shaking—and yanked me back up by one arm.

A man with a scruffy-looking yellow beard stepped out of the cabin door, blinked rapidly as though the light hurt his eyes, and yelled, "Where ya been? Everyone's waiting."

"You wanted him sooner, maybe you should'a grabbed him yourself," Beer Belly snarled.

The figure in front of the cabin glanced fearfully over his shoulder. "You shouldn't be saying things like that in front of Mr. Blackburn."

"Well, we couldn't exactly snatch him until he got knocked over the head," the leader muttered, but I could tell his heart wasn't in it. "Come on," he said, yanking my arm. "Let's get him inside."

The cabin had two small windows in the front and one on the side. Dark curtains were drawn across all of them, leaving the inside lit only by the flames of flickering candles set around the room. After the bright day outside, I could barely see a thing as I was pushed through the door.

"Seat him here," said a voice that seemed almost reptilian in its whispering hiss. I knew that voice. It was the figure I'd seen the night before in the woods. I thought I'd be less freaked out seeing him here instead of in the woods, but as I was pushed into a chair and faced him across a rough wooden table, he looked every bit as ghostlike as I'd remembered.

"Who are you?" I asked, trying to keep my voice from shaking.

"A question not nearly as important as who *you* are." He steepled his fingers beneath his chin and watched me with eyes that seemed to mirror the flickering candles with an interior flame of their own. "But since I intend to learn a great deal about you, I will introduce myself. I am the eyes that see all. I am the finger that calls down the stars of heaven and sends them flaming into the sea. I am alpha and omega. Id and ego. I bring death and life. I am the footstep you hear when the moon is full that makes you pull your head beneath the blankets, trembling."

I'm not going to lie. This dude scared the heck out of me. He was not only crazy, I was pretty sure he was dangerous. But I couldn't help smiling at the image that appeared in my mind at his words: Darkwing Duck, the Disney cartoon superhero who goes around in a purple cloak and mask.

"Let me guess," I said, unable to help myself. "You're also the terror that flaps in the night."

Apparently he didn't appreciate my joke. His face tightened as he looked around at the ten or so men and women standing and sitting around the room. "What are you still doing here?" As if snapped with a whip, they got to their feet and hustled out of the door.

He pointed to the two men standing on either side me. "Untie his hands and hold him against the table."

I turned to see the man on my right pull a huge knife from his belt, and a second later he cut through the ropes binding my wrists. The two men grabbed my hands and shoved them onto the table.

"Now we will see," said Blackburn. The moment his long white fingers touched my hands, I knew I was in trouble. Any lasting humor I still had disappeared as a burning sensation drilled from his fingertips into the backs of my hands, through my wrists, and up into my shoulders. My arms felt limp and dead—two hunks of wood on the scarred tabletop.

Blackburn's eyes glittered as he turned my hands palm up and traced his fingers over them. "Yes." He nodded slowly as if reading a good book. "Most interesting."

Around the room, the candles flickered, though there was no breeze. Blackburn's lips barely moved, but his voice was hard and clear. "I see a bear and an eagle locked in mortal combat."

I played for the Copper Hills Grizzlies, and we had been scheduled to play the Eagles the day after I came here.

"I see winding passageways from far away, and strange messengers from the land of the unseeing. I see doors that do not open, and mouths afraid to speak."

The tunnels, Ladan, the door, and yesterday in the church. How was he doing this?

When he looked up and grinned at me, his teeth seemed as sharp as the fangs of a snake. His hand shot out lightning-fast and reached into my pocket. Clutched between his fingers were my letters and resting on his palm, the key.

"Give me those," I said. I tried to yank away from the men holding me, but couldn't break their grip.

I expected Blackburn to read the letters. Instead, he touched them to the flame of a candle. As they burned, he moved the key from finger to finger, spinning it over his knuckles so that it moved rapidly left and right over the back of his hand. "The words of fools are dross. And gems turn to dust in their mouths."

I had no idea what he was talking about, but he absolutely terrified me. This was no fake, no twenty-dollar fortune-teller. I'd never felt evil like I felt in that room. It radiated from him like heat from a roaring fire.

"Smith has the treasure. But I *will* get it." He closed the key in his fingers, and for a moment I thought I saw something gray move in his fist. The movement was too quick and subtle to make out even with my improved eyesight. I was reminded again of a magician.

I tried to speak, but my lips were numb. All I could do was shake my head.

"Oh, yes. And you *will* help me." He uncurled his fist. The only thing in his palm was the key. If he'd been holding something else, it was gone. "Like a fly in a spider's web, you have become entangled in a very dangerous trap. And the only chance you have of getting out is by helping me." He laid the key flat on the table where its black surface matched his dark eyes.

As long as he was touching me, I felt frozen in place. But the moment he released his grip, I dropped my shoulder and rammed the man to my right in the gut. Before he could react, I elbowed the guy on my left. Terror filled me with a crazy energy. I snatched the key from the table, rocked my chair over backward, and somersaulted toward the door.

Ramming it open, I raced out into the bright light of day. Leaving the room felt like escaping a coffin. I expected

Blackburn to come after me—to send his men with their knives and guns. What I heard as I ran across the road and into the trees was even more chilling. The man who had so accurately divined so much about me was laughing. His voice seemed to fill earth and air as he shouted with glee.

"Run as fast as your feet will carry you, boy. When you spend the last of your energy, I will be waiting for you."

Had I learned what I was sent here to find out? I didn't know for sure. But one thing I did know was that I didn't want to stay around any longer. I wanted to find the last part of the key and get the heck out of Dodge—or Palmyra in this case. If I still had anything I needed to be taught, I would be more than happy to learn the rest of it in seminary. In fact, if I could just get out of here in one piece I would go to seminary every day for the rest of the year, and next year. I'd even go twice a day just so long as I didn't have to have anything more to do with Alistair Blackburn and his creepy eyes.

CHAPTER 19

Branches slapped at my hands and face as I ran through the trees. I was sure Blackburn's men would show up any minute, and I couldn't shake the feeling I was reliving my first night here all over again. Would they shoot me? They needed me alive if they thought I could help them get the plates. But that didn't mean they needed me uninjured. The crazy thing was that I still wasn't sure I believed the plates were real.

I spotted a trail through the woods and followed it until I was exhausted. When I couldn't run another step, I collapsed against a big rock and was not surprised in the least to realize this was the same rock I'd been hiding behind when Joseph had come running through the trees with the plates. I was nearly back where I'd started.

What now? I couldn't return to the hotel. Everyone would be looking for me there. And I couldn't get back through the door without the last piece of the key. I was sure Joseph's family would welcome me if I went there, but that was just putting off the inevitable. I had to get the last piece of the key, and to do that I needed help.

Looking down at the trail I'd followed the night I came through the door, I realized there was only one person I could go to for help. Jennie had asked me to meet her at her house. I didn't want to get her into the same trouble I was wrapped up in, but I didn't have anywhere else to go.

It wasn't hard to find the hill I'd rolled down after getting shot. From there, it was a short walk to the Jaggers' house. Halfway across the field, I squatted down, looking for any signs of movement. I wasn't sure how Jennie's mom would react to seeing me. I knew I didn't want to run into her dad.

From the other side of a wooden fence, a big black-and-white cow eyed me curiously before returning to chewing grass. In front of the Jaggers' house a handful of chickens milled about, pecking and clawing at the dirt. A goat, tied to a rail, kicked and bleated. I counted to a hundred, but there was no sign of any people inside or outside the house.

Cautiously I made my way across the field, ready to run back into the woods at the first sign of danger. By the time I reached the front yard, sweat was pouring down my back, and I was dying for a drink of water. When I was a little more than ten feet away from the porch, I whistled. There was no sign of movement behind the windows. Was it a trap? Were they waiting until I was too close to escape before charging out the door?

"Jennie," I called. My voice seemed loud enough to carry for miles in the still air, but still no one came out. I knew I couldn't stand there forever. So, with my heart racing, I crossed the front porch and knocked on the door. There was no answer. Peeking through the windows, I discovered the house was empty.

She *had* told me to meet her here. But that was before her father had hit me over the head. I walked around the back of the house and into the small barn, expecting at any minute for someone to burst out of hiding. The barn was as empty as the house, and a small outbuilding held only tools and some bags of seed.

For whatever reason, everyone in the Jagger household was gone. Now what should I do? I was sure I was alone, so I didn't look up as I came around the front of the house. It wasn't until a shadow dropped over me that I saw the man on horseback a few feet in front of me. He had a scruffy gray beard and a tall black hat with a curved top. The stock of a rifle extended from a leather scabbard on the side of his saddle.

I looked up into his eyes, too scared to run. He tugged on his beard.

"You must be Kaleo."

□　□　□

"How did you know you could find me here?" I asked, once I was sure he wasn't one of Blackburn's men or someone working for Jennie's dad.

Major Obadiah Dickerson, as he'd introduced himself to me, tugged at the tip of his beard. "I didn't. I asked around and heard you'd been staying at the hotel. The Westleys hadn't seen you since this morning. But someone said you'd spent the night here before checking into the hotel. So I thought I'd stop by and see if the Jaggers might know where to find you. Now here you are."

"Here I am," I agreed.

Major Dickerson pulled off his hat and fished around inside before pulling something out. "I imagine you've been waiting for this?"

The last letter! He had no idea.

"Nice fellow gave it to me about a week or so ago. Said he expected you'd be around for it sooner or later."

I took the envelope from him with shaking hands. "Do I owe you anything?" I asked. "Some kind of delivery charge?"

"Nope." He pulled his hat back tight on his head and reined his horse around. "All taken care of. You be safe, now."

I watched him ride down the road—his horse's hooves kicking up small plumes of dirt—before turning the letter over in my hands. The last one. I shook the envelope, listening to the soft *chik-chik* of the final key piece sliding around inside.

With the tip of my finger, I slipped the envelope open.

Kaleo,

If you are reading this letter you are nearing the end of your journey. You have sought the knowledge you need and now you must determine if you have the faith to use it. Listen to your heart and return home with honor.

From one witness to another,

Jadan

Had I gained the knowledge I was sent to receive? I'd definitely learned a lot. And I had plenty to think about. What was the faith to use it though? I wasn't sure I did have the faith. But if I'd made it to the end of my journey, I must.

I looked toward the Jaggers' house, wishing I could see Jennie one last time. It didn't feel right leaving without saying good-bye to her. But what choice did I have? If I didn't leave soon, Blackburn would catch up to me. The memory of his eyes and his words still chilled me.

Tucking the letter into my pocket, I started across the field. As I walked, I took the key from my jacket. It had a greasy feel to it, as if Blackburn had somehow contaminated it simply by touching the metal. But at least nothing appeared damaged. I fitted the last piece onto the end. *Knowledge is the key, and faith the power to turn it.* The words circled around and around in my mind. I thought about what Joseph Smith had said: "Knowledge does away with darkness, suspense, and doubt; for these cannot exist where knowledge is."

Had I done away with my doubt? I wanted to say I had, but inside I wasn't sure. If I still had doubt, did that mean I didn't yet have enough knowledge, or that I didn't have enough faith? Why was I even still thinking about it? I had the key. I could open the door and go home. That's what I'd wanted all along. And I wanted it even more now that I'd come face-to-face with one of the most evil men I could imagine.

"You don't need to be here anymore," I told myself. "Go home. Get on with your life."

It was good advice. Ladan had sent me here and now he was bringing me home. Who was I to argue? With the finished key tucked securely in my pocket, I trudged up the hill and followed the trail until it led me to the door in the side of the hill.

"Knowledge and faith," I whispered. Knowledge and faith. It was crazy, but a part of me didn't want to leave—didn't think I was *ready* to leave. It was just not being able to say good-bye to Jennie, I told myself.

Realizing I was putting off the inevitable, I slid the key into the lock. It clicked into place and I swallowed. "Okay, let's get this over with."

With a deep breath, I turned the key. Nothing happened. I turned it again. It spun easily in the lock. Too easily, like pedaling a bike with no chain. Something was wrong. I pulled the key out and studied it. All four pieces were locked together. What was I missing?

Once again, I pushed the key into the lock and turned. There was no friction, no sense of anything moving inside. I grabbed the knob and tried to turn it. It wouldn't budge. I pounded on the wood—my fists echoing.

Behind me the woods filled with laughter. I spun around to find Blackburn leaning against a tree, watching me with a pleased expression on his face. His lips pulled back in a wicked sneer as he roared with amusement. "I told you, you couldn't leave."

I looked toward the woods behind me, wondering if his men were hidden, waiting for me to make a break for it.

"Where will you go?" Blackburn asked, running his fingers over his strange black-and-white beard. "The door won't open, even with your key."

"What did you do?" I asked. "Did you break it somehow?"

Blackburn chuckled again. "I do wish I could take credit for your misfortunes, but I'm afraid that belongs to someone else. To be perfectly honest, I can't even see the door myself. But I know it's there. I can sense it. And as soon as you help me with my problem, I'll help you with yours."

I backed against the door. "You're crazy if you think I'll help you steal the plates."

"I was afraid you'd say that," Blackburn sighed. "I suppose I'll have to let you deal with that pesky door yourself then."

"Wait!" I called as he started to turn away. He was right. I had nowhere else to turn. What was I doing wrong? I swallowed. "How do I know you can help me? You could be lying just to get the plates."

"I *could* be." He moved from the tree and took a step toward me. I edged sideways. "In fact, I wouldn't put it past me at all. But in this case my offer is quite verifiable."

He reached into his pocket and I got ready to sprint, expecting a gun or a knife. What he pulled out was neither, but it froze me in place, just the same. Dangling from his fingertips was a letter.

A letter from Ladan.

Have you ever thought you knew someone really well? Considered them a close friend? Then you discover they've been keeping something from you, and you have to question everything they've ever done or said. It hurts. A lot.

CHAPTER 20

That's impossible. I found all the letters. The last one I read said it was the final piece." I held out the key. The pieces came all the way to the tip. There was no room to add another one.

"Indeed." Blackburn chuckled. "I imagine it *was* the final piece. But that assumes you got all the pieces before it. Unfortunately you missed one."

I looked down at the key and a horrible empty feeling filled my chest. I'd assumed the first letter contained the first piece of the key. It hadn't slid quite all the way to the handle, but I thought that was the way the key was made. Now I could see there was a groove for one more piece at the base of the rod. That's why the key wouldn't work.

"It's really quite a simple bargain I'm proposing," Blackburn said. "Tonight you will go to the Smith farm, where you will watch young Joseph hide the plates. It shouldn't be hard. He trusts you. After he goes to bed, you will send us a signal, and we will retrieve the treasure."

"How can I trust you?"

"You can't, of course." He tilted his head, tore open the envelope and dropped the last piece of the key into his palm. Obviously enjoying every moment of my frustration, he tossed the tiny piece of metal up into the air and caught it. He nearly dropped it, and I couldn't stop myself from gasping. How long would it take to find the piece if it fell into the tall grass? What if it got lost, barring me from returning home forever?

I thought about the Smiths. How nice they'd been at dinner. How could I betray them? What choice did I have, though? I had to get the last piece of the key. If Joseph really was a prophet, he'd find a way to get the plates back. If God really wanted the Book of Mormon to be published, it would. I bit my lip, my fingernails cutting into my palms as I clenched my fists.

Blackburn wasn't a big man. Maybe I could charge him. Grab the key and get through the door before he could call for help.

Before I finished the thought, six strong men stepped out from the trees. I recognized most of them from the cabin. They were all holding pistols or rifles, and smiling.

"Fine," I said, defeated. "But I don't want any of your tricks. I'm not telling you where the plates are until you give me the key." Maybe there was still a way to get the key and escape, without betraying Joseph's trust.

"I don't think so." Blackburn shook his head. "These men

will accompany you to get the plates, and they will accompany you as you bring them to me. Once I have the treasure, I will give you the key." He tossed the tiny black piece high into the air. I watched it spin nearly to the branches, and I was sure he was going to drop it this time. With a deft move that reminded me of a magician pulling handkerchiefs out of thin air, he caught the piece and made it disappear up his sleeve.

"One other thing," he said. "Perhaps you think you can escape and find another way through the door. Who am I to say it's not possible? I understand you have the curious ability to survive wounds you shouldn't. I'd like to learn more about that sometime. But for now, remember this. You may be impervious to harm. But some others aren't so lucky."

He nodded his head to the right, and I turned to see two men step out of the trees. They were holding a struggling figure between them. The figure was bound and gagged but I recognized her at once. It was Jennie.

So far I'd been able to keep my temper under control, but seeing Jennie scared and pale—her hands tied, and a gag stuffed into her mouth—accomplished what even the thought of losing the key hadn't. "Leave her alone!" I charged toward the two men, but before I could get halfway there, Blackburn was standing beside them, a long gleaming knife at Jennie's throat.

"Tut, tut," he said. "Save your energy for tonight."

"Let her go," I growled. Jennie's frightened eyes went back and forth between Blackburn and me. I couldn't do anything to help her.

"I will—as soon as I have the plates," Blackburn said.

"No." My arms and legs trembled with rage. "She has nothing to do with this. You don't need her. You already have the key."

"Call it insurance. Although I must say, I can't understand why you feel so strongly about what happens to her after the way she's treated you." He looked at Jennie and something passed silently between the two of them. I tried to catch her eyes, but she looked away.

"What are you talking about?"

Blackburn rubbed the tip of one finger slowly across the envelope he was still holding. It made a smooth *shhh* sound, like the hiss of a snake. "Aren't you even curious," he asked, glancing toward Jennie, who was now staring at her feet, "where I got this letter? Haven't you wondered why you received all the others, but not this one?"

I turned from him to Jennie, the meaning of his words sinking in. "No. I don't believe it. You're lying."

"I only wish I was," he said, putting a hand to his chest. "Young love is such a delicate thing. So fragile. So tender. Hearts are so quickly lost and so easily broken. Alas, I'm afraid your dear little Jennie had the letter all along. Had it, and refused to give it to you."

I shook my head slowly back and forth.

He turned to Jennie. "Tell him yourself. Gentlemen, would you be so kind as to remove the young lady's gag."

With a growing sense of dread, I watched the two thugs on either side of Jennie untie the cloth and pull the gag roughly from her mouth. It couldn't be true. Jennie was the one person here who had believed me. The one person I was sure I could trust. She wouldn't have done something like that to me. But when she finally looked up, her eyes were filled with tears.

"Tell them you didn't do it," I said.

"I'm sorry." Her voice was barely a whisper.

I would rather have been blindsided midfield by a safety than have to listen to those two words. "Why?"

She shook her head, tears pouring down her cheeks. I wanted to wipe them away, but I felt frozen to the ground. "At first . . . I didn't know. I saw those men who fixed our fence give my father the letter. I didn't know what it was about or why they gave it to him. Then the thing with the saw happened, and he was sure they were practicing black magic. He made them leave. I forgot all about the letter until you came along."

Overhead the wind began to blow, and dead leaves dropped from the braches, spinning to the ground like fallen soldiers. "I should have known you weren't like my father said. And I did once I talked to you outside the church. That's when I took the letter from the mantel where I knew he'd hidden it. I was going to give it to you this morning, only . . ." Jennie sniffed and forced herself to meet my eyes. "I didn't want you to leave."

I felt like I'd been kicked in the stomach. "So you gave it to them instead?"

"No!" She glared at Blackburn, a little of the fire I remembered coming back into her eyes. "I was going to give it to you this afternoon. I swear. But they came to the house and kidnapped me before I could do it."

Blackburn waved the blade near Jennie's throat. "This is all very sweet. But we have no more time for these theatrics. My proposition is simple. You give me the plates; I give you the last piece of the key. The girl goes free. What you two lovebirds do after that is really none of my business."

What choice did I have? "Fine. But if you try to pull any kind of trick, I swear you'll be sorry."

Blackburn flicked the knife with the tiniest twist of his wrist. It flew through the air—a blur of silver and black—and embedded itself in a tree trunk nearly thirty feet away with a solid thunk.

"You are the one who will be sorry if you do not do exactly as you are told. You might think you can fool me—that I am an old man, and my wits may be fading. But let me assure you, if I do not have the gold Bible in my hands by sunrise tomorrow, you will pay a price you can't possibly imagine. If you betray me, I promise that you will spend the rest of your life regretting that decision."

He spun on the heel of one sharp-toed black boot and pointed to the trees. "Now get out of here."

I thought the worst feeling was having someone you thought you could trust hurt you. I was wrong. The worst feeling is being the one who betrays someone who thought they could trust you.

CHAPTER 21

Well, this is a surprise." Emma stood at the door with a wide grin on her face. She was wearing an apron and had a smear of flour on her right cheek. Her dark hair was pulled up into a bun. "Mother," she called over her shoulder, "Kaleo is here."

"Invite him in," Mother Smith said.

As I walked through the door, the smell of something wonderful nearly made me forget why I was there.

"Couldn't get enough of Mother's cooking?" called Hyrum who was sitting at the table working on what looked like a leather horse bridle. "Or was it the Smith family charm that brought you back?"

"Ignore him," Emma said, waving a hand that was also white with flour. "It doesn't matter why you're here. I didn't get a chance to thank you properly for your help last night. When those men showed up, I didn't know what we were going to do."

"Don't thank me," I said, guilt at my real reason for coming making me sick to my stomach. "Joseph was the one who came up with the idea."

"Joseph isn't scared of anything," Lucy said, skipping down the stairs.

"I know," Emma said, with a frown. "And sometimes that worries me."

"No need for you to worry." Hyrum playfully flexed a muscle. "He has his big brother to protect him."

"Why doesn't that make me feel any better?" Emma kidded back.

"I hope you're staying for dinner," Mother Smith said, as she began spooning hot golden balls of dough out of a pot onto a clean cloth.

I swallowed. "Actually, I need to speak with Joseph. Is he around?"

"He's out chopping wood," Emma said. "I was just about to take him some corn dodgers and cold milk. But you can go if you like. Feel free to have some yourself as well."

"If you get a chance." Hyrum pushed the tip of his nose into a pig snout and grinned.

Trying not to spill any of the milk from the metal pitcher, I walked across the back field until I saw Joseph hacking branches off a fallen pine with an axe. "Finally decided to come out and do some *real* work?" he called as I came up beside him.

"I, uh . . ." I muttered, still more than a little tongue-tied around the man I'd heard so much about.

"Oh," he said, turning around. "Sorry. I thought you were Hyrum." He spied the milk and the cloth bundle that steamed in the cool evening air. "Tell me those are Mother's corn dodgers."

I nodded, although, to be perfectly honest, I had no idea what a corn dodger was. Setting the axe aside, Joseph took the pitcher from me. He filled the dipper, tilted back his head, and emptied it in three quick gulps. "If they don't drink cold milk in heaven," he said, with a contented groan, "I'll have to file a complaint."

I grinned.

"Now then," he said, patting a spot on the log as he sat down. "Let's tuck into those dodgers."

It turns out that corn dodgers were kind of deep-fried bread with corn inside. Not as sweet or light as doughnut holes, but about the same size. I could have eaten them washed down with cold, fresh milk all night. When we'd finished everything Emma had sent, I wiped the milk from my upper lip with the back of my hand. "So *do* they?"

"Do they what?" Joseph swallowed the last of the milk and set the dipper into the empty pitcher.

"Drink milk in heaven?"

He tilted his head and gave me an odd look. I felt the blood rush to my face.

"I just thought, you know, since you'd talked to angels that . . ."

He folded his arms across his chest, threw back his head,

and burst out laughing. "I'm afraid that topic hasn't come up yet."

Feeling like a total idiot, I looked off into the trees. How did you talk to someone who claimed to have seen God and Jesus Christ?

Joseph laid his hand on my shoulder. "I'm guessing you didn't come here to talk about milk."

I shook my head, unable to look him in the eye. Guilt was tearing me up. "You're not what I expected," I finally said.

"You mean I'm even more handsome than the girls in town say?"

I looked down at my hands.

"Weak joke," he said with a sigh.

"That's what I'm talking about," I said. "I didn't expect you to tell jokes, or throw rolls, or chop wood. You're a prophet. I thought you'd be more . . . serious."

Joseph cupped his chin between his thumb and forefinger. I thought he might be mad because of what I'd said, but he didn't look angry, only thoughtful. "You suppose that a person who the Lord should see fit to reveal his will to must be something more than a man?"

"I guess."

He looked out toward the trees. "St. James said the prophet Elijah was a man—subject to the same passions as we are, yet he had such power with God that He, in answer to Elijah's prayers, shut the heavens that they gave no rain for the space of three years and six months. And again, in answer to his prayer, the heavens gave forth rain, and the earth gave forth

fruit. Indeed, such is the darkness and ignorance of this generation, that they look upon it as incredible that a man should
have any dealings with his Maker."

I'd never considered it that way before.

Joseph smiled softly. "I am but a man, Kaleo. People expect me to be perfect. If they expect perfection from me, I
should expect it from them too. But if they will bear with my
infirmities, I will likewise bear with theirs."

Again it struck me that Joseph was not much older than I
was. I'd made plenty of mistakes in my life. How would I feel if
everyone suddenly started expecting me to be perfect? "It must
be hard," I said. "Getting people to listen to you."

Joseph smiled and tapped a spot on the log. "Sometimes
getting anything through the heads of this generation is like
splitting hemlock knots with a corn dodger for a wedge and a
pumpkin for a mallet."

"Don't you ever . . . I don't know . . . Don't you ever just
want to quit trying? I mean, if people don't want to listen, it's
their problem, right?" As soon as I said the words, I realized I
was talking about myself. I was the one who didn't want to listen. I was the one who expected him to be more than a man. I
was the one who was as stubborn as a hemlock knot, whatever
that was. What I was asking was why he didn't give up on me.

Joseph gripped my arm. "Kaleo, I did see a light, and in the
midst of that light I saw two Personages, and they did in reality
speak to me; and though I am hated and persecuted for saying that I have seen a vision, yet it *is* true; and while they are
persecuting me, reviling me, and speaking all manner of evil

against me falsely for so saying, I am led to say in my heart: Why persecute me for telling the truth?"

All around us the woods seemed to go still. Joseph looked me in the eyes. "I have actually seen a vision; and who am I that I can withstand God, or why does the world think to make me deny what I have actually seen? For I have seen a vision; I know it, and I know that God knows it. I cannot deny it, neither dare I do it. By so doing I would offend God, and come under condemnation."

At that moment I felt the same thing I had when he was teaching in the dining room the night before. I'd thought he sounded older then. Now I understood it wasn't his age that was different. It was his mantle of authority. I might be listening to a man, but I was also listening to something much more. I was listening to a prophet.

◻   ◻   ◻

All through dinner I couldn't meet Joseph's eyes—or any of the other Smiths, for that matter. More than once I started to say something—to admit I was a total loser and had come to betray them. But how could I? If it was only about me, I would have told Blackburn to forget it—even if it meant never returning to my own time. But they had Jennie, and I was sure they were serious about hurting her, or worse, if I didn't come through.

Shortly after we'd finished eating, Joseph stood and walked to the fireplace.

"What is it, son?" his father asked as Joseph pulled back the loose stone on the fireplace.

"I have received a warning," Joseph said. He reached into the opening in the fireplace and pulled out the box I'd seen him put there the night before. "They are coming for the plates tonight. I must hide them somewhere else."

"I'm coming with you," Hyrum said, pushing back from the table.

"Me too," Don Carlos said.

"No." Joseph walked to the door, holding the box to his chest. "You two stay here and look after the family. I'll be back shortly."

"You can't go by yourself," Emma said. "It's too dangerous."

Joseph smiled at Emma. Then he looked directly at me and said, "All will be well." With that, he was out the door.

"We can't let him go out there by himself," Hyrum said. "Those scoundrels could be hiding anywhere."

My stomach was in knots. I knew where the scoundrel was. He was sitting right at this table eating their food. My gut lurched, and I jumped from the bench, knowing I was going to throw up. "I'm sorry," I blurted. "I have to go."

Before anyone could say a word, I charged out the door. I'd barely made it into the trees when everything I'd just eaten came rushing up. Clutching myself, I heaved and heaved, wishing I would just collapse on the ground and die. What would my family think if they knew where I was and what I was doing? What would Brother Mortensen think? And Ladan. How would he feel if he knew he'd sent back in time a person who would steal the gold plates and give them to a bunch of treasure seekers?

In the distance, a light went on in the window of a small cabin on the Smith's property. A figure walked in front of the window. I glanced back into the darkness across the road. I couldn't see them, but I knew Blackburn and his men were out there somewhere.

"Don't do this," I told myself. "It's bad enough you don't believe. Don't ruin it for everyone else too. If you take the plates, the Book of Mormon will never be translated."

But the only thing I could think of was Jennie with a knife to her throat. It was my fault she was involved in this. My fault her life was in danger. I couldn't turn my back on her.

Feeling like the biggest creep ever, I slunk across the Smith property until I reached the side of the cabin. Someone was clearly inside. I could hear him moving around. Every so often there came a *r-e-e-e-e* sound like a squeaky door. Slowly I lifted my head above the sill of the window.

Joseph was on the other side of the room. I could see his silhouette by the light of a small lantern hanging from the wall. I thought this might have been a house at one time, but now it looked like some kind of workshop. Strips of wood and various tools covered the tables. Metal hoops hung from the walls. A dozen or so barrels were stacked in one corner.

Rising up a little, I could see that Joseph was kneeling on the floor. He had a tool in his hand and was doing something I couldn't quite make out. As I watched, he leaned back and the *r-e-e-e-e* sound came again. He straightened, and I saw him lift a thin wooden plank from the floor. He moved back, revealing a dark opening, and I understood what was happening. He was pulling up floorboards. That's where he was going to hide the plates—under the floor of the cabin.

It was a brilliant idea. Blackburn's men could search the cabin all day and night and they'd never think to look there. Not unless . . . unless I told them. Around me the wind began to blow again. The moonlight disappeared, and I looked up to see dark low clouds moving in fast.

As though hefting a great weight, Joseph picked up the box from his side and lowered it into the hole. A light rain began to spatter the dry ground, and a darkness like nothing I'd ever known fell over me. I was going to do it. I was going to betray the prophet. Even if there was forgiveness for that—and I wasn't sure there was—I could never forgive myself. But I had to save Jennie.

Watching Joseph laying the boards back across the hole, I remembered what he'd said to me as we sat on the log: "Such is the darkness and ignorance of this generation, that they look upon it as incredible that a man should have any dealings with his Maker."

Could he have been talking about me? About my ignorance? Once I'd believed in prayer. But now I couldn't bring myself to accept that God would really listen to me—especially with what I was about to do. But who else did I have to turn to?

As the rain began to fall more heavily, I bowed my head, and called silently to God with all my heart. "Please help me,

Heavenly Father. I've totally messed things up. I know I haven't been going to church. I know I haven't had the faith to believe. I don't want to do this thing. But I can't let Jennie pay for my mistakes."

Overhead, lightning split the sky and thunder shook the ground. Joseph looked up from what he was doing and turned to stare directly at the window I was peeking though. The lantern was on the other side of the room; its light was nowhere near me. The night was so black I knew I had to be hidden from him, and yet he seemed to look straight into my eyes.

He tilted his head as though hearing an inner voice, and then reached into the hole. When he rose up again, I saw he was holding a cloth bundle almost exactly the same size and shape as the box. Tucking the bundle under one arm, he climbed a wooden ladder to a loft area just out of my sight. When he came back down, the bundle was gone.

Quickly he finished nailing the boards in place. After examining his work, he kicked sawdust around to hide what he'd done. A moment later, he snuffed out the lantern and left the cabin without another glance in my direction.

What did that mean? Obviously he had hidden the box under the floor. But what was the bundle he'd carried up to the loft?

Cold and dripping, I edged around the corner of the cabin and stared into the darkness. Was it a trick? Did he know I was watching him? With my improved vision, I could see the trees and bushes. But with no stars or moonlight, there were too many gray shapes. Joseph could be hiding a few feet away without me knowing. Going inside was the only way to find out for sure.

My heart was pounding so loud in my ears that I could barely hear the rain as I tiptoed to the entrance and lifted the latch. I eased the door open and slipped through. Total darkness engulfed me and I felt more vulnerable than ever. What if he had doubled back inside and was waiting to catch me in the act of taking the plates?

I waited for my eyes to adjust—for my super sight to kick in. After a minute or two, I realized even *my* eyes had limits. A candle would have come in handy. But I couldn't have used one even if I'd had it for fear of being seen. Shuffling my feet across the floor, I moved to where I remembered seeing the ladder. I'd check out the cloth bundle first, then pull up the floorboards if I had to. As my groping hands found the ladder and reached for the wooden rung, a thought occurred to me. What if there were no plates? What if it really was all a fake? Blackburn would never believe me if I came back empty-handed.

Something snapped outside the cabin and I froze. Waiting silently with one hand on the ladder, I listened for any sign of movement. At last, deciding it must have been the wind, I climbed carefully up to the loft. The area at the top of the ladder was not much more than a crawl space. If I stood straight up I'd hit my head. I crawled around the wooden floor, feeling in front of me as I went. I found four more barrels. But no cloth bundle.

For a second I wondered if I'd made a mistake. Maybe

Joseph had carried the bundle back down and I'd missed it. Then I bumped my shoulder against one of the barrels and realized that whatever Joseph had carried up here was hidden. Quickly I got to my feet and plunged my hand into the nearest barrel. It was filled with some kind of fibers, long and silky, soft as cotton balls. It was like plunging my hand into a pile of fine hair. I reached to the bottom, but there was nothing but the fibers. The next barrel was the same.

Worried that Blackburn would do something to Jennie if I didn't hurry, I thrust my hands into the next barrel. Instantly I touched something out of place. A hard rectangle. I ran my hands around the lump and recognized the cloth covering I'd seen Joseph holding. It was heavier than I'd expected—forty or fifty pounds at least. It took both hands to pull it free of its downy hiding place.

My hands were damp and clammy as I set the bundle on the wooden floor in front of me and knelt over it. Suddenly scared to death of what I might find, I lifted back the cloth. As I brushed against the object inside, I heard a metallic fluttering sound like a pair of tin pie pans brushing against each other or . . . or metal plates.

Just as I pulled back the final fold of cloth, lightning struck outside the cabin. For a brief second the inside of the cabin lit up and I caught a quick glimpse of what was before me. It was a rectangle the size of a big hardcover book—a math book maybe. It was at least six-inches thick and bound with three gold rings. In the lightning's flash, it gleamed a lustrous gold, and I saw tiny symbols scratched into the surface.

My throat squeezed down to the size of a straw. It was the plates. The gold plates were real, and they were lying on the floor right in front of me.

As the light disappeared, the door to the cabin slammed open with a bang and a voice hissed, "I saw you come in here. Now, show yourself."

There are certain points in your life when you make decisions you can never turn back from. It's like crossing the street for the first time—looking left and right before stepping out. Only in this case you know that once you cross that street, it's for good. You can't ever go back. All you can do is hope you made the correct decision.

CHAPTER 22

My first thought was that Joseph had seen me and returned to the cabin. But a second later, I recognized the voice, and the stink of sweat and whiskey that floated across the air with it.

"Light a lantern," said a second voice.

"Are you plum crazy?" said the first voice. "Do you want to get caught?"

Quickly I wrapped the cloth back around the plates.

"Get out here, boy, if you want to see your girlfriend alive."

It sounded like Beer Belly and his good friend Long-tall-and-ugly. Realizing they couldn't see me any more than I could see them, I returned the plates to the barrel and climbed silently down the ladder. "Be quiet," I whispered. "Do you want to bring the whole Smith family?"

Dumb but not stupid, they waited while I felt my way across the room. With my eyes adjusted a little more to the darkness, I could see there were more than just the two of them. Five or six figures were huddled inside the door to the cabin or just outside. I looked for Blackburn, but he must have stayed back.

"Do you have it?" Beer Belly asked—the greed was clear in his voice.

"Where's Jennie?" I asked.

Shorty's laugh sounded like the whinny of a horse. "You can have your girlfriend once you give us the plates."

"Let me see her." I wondered if they'd brought her at all, or if it was another trick, but Beer Belly signaled to someone outside. A moment later a man with a chest-length beard brought Jennie through the door. She was tied and gagged, but that didn't stop her from struggling. I couldn't help admiring her bravery. If it had been me in her position—with my life depending on the actions of someone I barely knew—I'd have been doing everything I could not to wet my pants.

"There," Beer Belly said, "you see her. Now where are the plates?"

I glanced over my shoulder to the loft. I'd seen the plates. Joseph had been telling the truth all along. Could I give them up?

I turned around at the sound of a struggle. Jennie had pulled away from the man holding her and was squirming left and right. He tried to get her under control, but she pulled her hands up to her mouth and managed to yank part of the gag free.

"Don't do it. Don't give it to them."

The man holding her raised his hand to hit her and I

stepped forward and caught his wrist. "Touch her and this ends." I squeezed his arm until I could feel the bones starting to move. He pulled back, his face pale under the scraggly beard.

"I don't have any choice," I said, turning to Jennie.

She shook her head and I could see her wet eyes glittering. "I don't understand what all of this is about. But if you believe Joe Smith—if you believe he really saw an angel and talked with God—you can't do anything against him. You can't. What would that make you?"

If you believe he really saw an angel and talked with God . . . Did I? Did I believe it? I thought about the plates hidden above me. More than that, I thought about the conversations I had had with Joseph. The things he said. He didn't come off as a man seeking fame, fortune, or power. He wasn't a bragger or a con man. He seemed like an honest human being who'd experienced an incredible vision and was trying his best to live up to the great responsibilities placed on his shoulders.

Did I believe him? *Knowledge is the key, and faith the power to turn it.*

Despite the wind and rain, a hot ball filled my chest and began to grow. It was a feeling I hadn't had in a long, long time. A feeling I hardly recognized at first. It was the Holy Ghost witnessing that what I'd seen and heard was true. I *did* believe Joseph. I believed everything. Those plates hidden in the loft were the word of God written by prophets. And Joseph Smith was the first of many prophets who would take part in spreading that word. I did more than believe it. I *knew* it.

I met Jennie's eyes. "Where's Blackburn?"

"He doesn't get his own hands dirty," Beer Belly grunted. "Not that it matters to you. Now, are you going to give us the plates, or do you want to see the girl die?"

I knew what I had to do. "I'll tell you where the plates are if you let her go."

Beer Belly wore an expression I couldn't read. Was he up to something? He turned to Sally, the only women in his group. "She's got a peep stone. Lie and she'll know it."

I swallowed. "They're here, in the cabin. But they're hidden. I won't tell you where until you release Jennie."

Beer Belly's eyes gleamed as he turned to Sally. She pulled something out of her dress pocket. Outside the rain had stopped and the moon gleamed silver. In its light, I could see the green stone she'd showed me before. She held it up to her eye and everyone held their breath as she looked slowly around the inside of the small cabin.

A grin split her face as she took the peep stone from her eye. "He's telling the truth. It's here, close by."

Beer Belly turned to the man holding Jennie. "Cut her free." He glared at me. "But you ain't going anywhere until I have the plates in my hands."

"Then you'll give me the key?"

He chuckled. "Sure. Then we'll give you the key."

I didn't know if they'd ever planned on giving it to me, but they never would now. I was going to be trapped in this time forever. But I'd made my decision. As long as Jennie was safe, I could live with what happened after.

Once they'd released her and pushed her out the door, I

looked down at the floorboards. "It's there," I said. "Under the floor. But he buried it pretty deep so you'll need to do some digging."

□   □   □

Nearly eight hours later, the floor of the Smith cabin was in shambles. Floorboards were strewn everywhere. Huge craters marked the ground beneath and dirt was piled up to the table-tops in some places. There'd been a lot of excitement when the box was found. But once they discovered it was empty, emotions went downhill quickly.

As the sun began to peek over the tops of the trees to the east, the sweaty men cursed one another and me most of all.

"We got to get out of here," Shorty said.

"Not without them plates." Beer Belly scowled at me. "Think you're smart, don't you?"

I held out my hands, palms up. "All I can tell you is that I saw him bring the box out here and bury it. Can I help it if the plates weren't inside?"

"Maybe he never had them in the first place," Long-tall-and-ugly said.

Beer Belly wiped a dirt-encrusted hand across his sweaty face, leaving a long dark smear. He looked over at Sally who had been sulking in the corner of the room ever since the box was found to be empty.

The sound of footsteps pounding across the ground outside made us all turn. The cabin door swung open and a boy who looked to be fourteen or fifteen darted inside. "They're awake," he said, puffing. "I seen one of 'em walk in front of the window, and there's smoke coming from the chimney."

Beer Belly spun on one boot heel. He glared at me before kicking the empty wooden box across the room with an angry curse. "Let's get out of here," he said. "But bring him. I can't wait until Blackburn gets through with him."

There was no point in trying to put up a fight. They had me well outnumbered. I'd known all along that I would have to face Blackburn again. But that didn't keep my legs from shaking as they tied my wrists and led me out of the cabin and through some trees to the waiting wagon. I'd managed to trick these punks, but somehow I didn't think Blackburn would believe my story quite as easily.

Although I was terrified of what was going to happen, I couldn't help feeling proud of myself. I'd made a lot of mistakes in my life, but in the end I'd done the right thing. Even if it cost me the chance to get home, I could look Joseph in the eye if and when I saw him again. Had he known I was there the night before? Had he given me the chance to do what was right, knowing I'd make the right choice, even when I hadn't known it myself?

A few minutes later, all those thoughts disappeared from my head as Beer Belly pulled the wagon up in front of Blackburn's cabin. Blackburn was standing outside the door. He didn't look happy.

"Well?" he said, before the wagon had even stopped rolling. "Did you get the treasure?"

Beer Belly scratched the back of his neck. "Smith must have known we was coming. He buried an empty box."

"Is that right?" Blackburn met my eyes, and I felt my gut go tight. "How could he possibly have known? Unless our guest warned him."

I tried to swallow, but my throat was too dry. "I didn't tell him anything. I didn't need to. I guess we know who the real prophet is. And who is the fraud."

Blackburn jerked backward. His face went tight. "Take him to the pond," he growled.

Horror blazed through my chest as the men grabbed me and yanked me over the side of the wagon. The *pond?* Did Blackburn somehow know water terrified me? If he'd realized I could recover from injuries, maybe his solution was to drown me.

Sweat slicked my face and ran down the middle of my back as the men dragged me across the field and dropped me to the ground a few feet away from a small dock that jutted out over the pond. My heart raced as I saw what was on the end of the small wooden structure: a big dark anvil. The kind I'd seen in the Smith cabin and in Mr. Jagger's blacksmith shop. There was a small, round ring welded to the top, and connected to the ring was ten feet or so of thick, coiled chain. It was an anchor.

Three of the men held me in place by my shoulders as Blackburn walked to the edge of the dock and laughed nastily. "Insightful to the end. I see you've figured out what I have in mind."

"I did what you wanted," I croaked. "I followed him and told you where he went."

Blackburn rubbed the scars on the side of his head. "You are a poor liar. You double-crossed me, and I told you what I do to people who betray me."

"At least you didn't get the plates," I said, trying to sound braver than I was feeling.

"Not yet. But we *will* get them. We'll just have to do it without you."

For the first time that day, I managed to smile. "If you know as much about me as you think you do, you know I'm telling the truth when I say you will never get the plates from Joseph Smith. He's going to translate them. The Book of Mormon is going to come out and people all over the world will read it and believe it. Millions of people. Even dumb kids as stubborn as me."

Shorty started to bray laughter, but instantly stopped when Blackburn turned his withering gaze on him. Blackburn knew I was right—I could see it in his face—but there was nothing he could do about it.

"So you're going to kill me?" I asked, no longer even trying to pretend I was brave.

"Not at all." Now it was Blackburn's turn to smile. I liked that even less than his snarl. "I promised you that if you lied to me, I would make sure you never forgot it. Death is too easy, too quick. You are going to be trapped here a long, long time. I want something for you to think about every day of your wretched life."

He walked up to the anvil and picked up a heavy metal lock. I didn't know what he was planning, but a terrible feeling came over me. What could be worse than death?

"When we were in the cabin," he said, holding out the lock, "I took the opportunity to make a wax impression of your key."

I remembered the greasy feel of the metal after he'd held it and the gray flash I thought I'd seen when he pressed it into his palm. Why would he do that?

"I had a copy made—with one small change." He plucked the last piece of the key from his jacket pocket and turned it slowly in his fingers. "*My* copy includes the last piece. If I hadn't destroyed it, I'm sure the key would have opened your door."

"Destroyed it?" I gulped. "You made a key only to get rid of it? What's the point?"

He grinned even wider. "The point is that I had this lock fitted to the key before I destroyed it. Had you delivered the plates to me and earned the last piece, which only I posses, your key could have opened this lock as well as the door."

I stared silently at him, with no idea of what he was up to, but knowing it had to be bad.

"Both the key and the lock were created for me at no charge by Abel Jagger. He felt he owed me a favor for removing a problem from his life, a thorn in his side. You, to be exact. Quite ironic when you think about it." His eyes flickered to something behind my shoulder and I spun around as the meaning of his words sunk in.

Standing behind me, bound and gagged, Jennie was gripped by the rest of Blackburn's crew. It wasn't me they were going to drown. As Blackburn had said, that was too easy.

They were going to kill her.

If you could give your life to save someone else's, would you? Before today, I would have said, "No. Definitely not." I'm willing to give my money, a ride, part of my lunch. But your life . . . I mean you've only got one of those. It wasn't until that moment I realized that some things are even more important.

CHAPTER 23

No!" I screamed, struggling to get to my feet, but with three big men pinning me, I couldn't budge.

"Did you really think we'd let her go?" Blackburn smiled a wide, terrifying grin. "Your friend knows far too much. We couldn't allow her to live. And when you think about it, it all works out quite well. She disappears, and you—the mysterious stranger—are the last one she was seen with. You'll tell your side of the story, of course, but I have a dozen witnesses who will vouch for the fact that we were all fifty miles from here, and another who will swear he saw you push something into the pond this morning.

"I imagine it won't be hard to put two and two together. You came to steal the plates all along. You befriended the Smith family and then turned on them. When you ransacked their cabin, without success, you became enraged and killed the only friend you had. Her father is the only one who might have a clue of the truth, but do you think he'll admit anything after they drag her body out of the pond and he realizes he made the very lock that took her life?"

I was shaking with rage, but I couldn't move an inch. "Kill me instead. She won't say anything."

"I'm afraid not." Blackburn motioned the men forward, and they dragged Jennie to the edge of the pier where Blackburn wrapped the chains tightly around her waist and snapped the lock closed. Leering at her, he turned the last piece of the key in his hand. "Of course you could save her," he said to me, "*if* you had this. But you made your choice."

As Blackburn leaned over and picked up a heavy metal mallet, Jennie glanced in my direction. Her eyes met mine and I saw something there. She looked quickly down at herself, raised her tied hands to her neck, then looked back at me. Was she trying to tell me something? If so, I had no idea what it was.

Blackburn hefted the mallet and set the final key piece on the anvil. "Say good-bye to your future," he said and brought the mallet down with a crash. It crushed the small piece completely. "Throw her in," he said to the men holding Jennie. For a minute they looked at each other, unsure.

"Don't do it!" I screamed. "Do you want to be murderers as well as thieves? He's just trying to save himself."

Blackburn turned the full power of his will on the men. As he spoke, his voice was soft, but his eyes burned. "Throw her in—now."

Like zombies, the three men hefted the anvil. It took all of their strength to lift it off the dock. Jennie looked at me one last time, her hands clasped to her chest, her eyes trying to convey a message I couldn't understand. The men heaved together, and the anvil dropped into the murky water with a green splash. Jennie was pulled in after it.

With a strength I didn't know I had, I threw the men off me and jumped to my feet. I strained at the ropes binding my wrists, but they were too tight.

"Cut him loose," Blackburn called with a laugh as he walked past me. "Let him try to free her without the last piece to his key. Maybe he'll drown along with her."

One of the men holding me pulled out a knife. As he cut the bonds from my wrists, I heard Blackburn shouting, "Let's go. We have to get out of town before anyone sees us."

As soon as the ropes fell from my hands, I raced to the end of the dock. The water was green and murky. As I stood perched above it, terrible thoughts and images filled my head. I could barely swim. I had no idea how deep the pond was or what might be at the bottom. I tried to make myself move, but my legs were paralyzed with fear. A burst of bubbles rose up from the depths. Something stirred the water. A second later, Jennie's face broke the surface.

"Kaleo!" she screamed, her hands paddling desperately. She tried to swim toward the dock, but the chain held her fast. "Help me," she cried, coughing and gagging.

It was her wide, terrified eyes that finally forced me into action. I was the reason she was in danger of dying. It was up to me to save her. I sucked in a deep breath and dived into the water.

It was impossible to see through the green murk. Pulling forward with long strokes, I prayed I could somehow find a way to free her.

It seemed like forever before my fingers touched the cold metal of the chain. Quickly I traced it to where it wrapped around Jennie's waist. I could feel her kick and struggle, trying to stay afloat. I yanked at the chains, but they were too tight. I couldn't get them off.

Hoping she understood I wasn't leaving her, I pulled myself hand-over-hand along the chain back to the anvil. *Be strong,* I thought to myself and to Jennie. But when I tried to lift the anvil, I found that I couldn't move it at all. It was slick with mud and nearly buried in the soupy bottom of the pond.

I couldn't lift the anvil and I couldn't get the chain off her. Pain burned my chest. I had to have air. Trying to fight off panic, I kicked for the surface. I broke through the water a few feet away from Jennie.

"I can't move the anvil," I choked.

She yelled something back, but my head slipped under the water and I swallowed a mouthful of pond. Fear sucked the energy from my arms and legs. Churning my feet, I managed to gasp in another breath of air.

"The lock." Jennie coughed. "You have to open the lock."

"I can't," I yelled. "The key won't work."

Jennie's head disappeared under the slime-covered water, and my throat closed. Then she was up again, reaching toward me. I could barely keep myself afloat, but I took her hand anyway. I'd do anything I could to keep her alive as long as I had the strength.

I felt her press something into my fingers. It was a small silver chain—the necklace she'd been wearing. "No." I tried to push it away. I didn't want gifts. I wanted to save her life. As I pressed my fingers against the chain, I felt something hanging from the end of it. It was small and hard, a little sharp and . . .

"Hurry," she gasped, pulling her hand out of my grip in order to keep treading water.

The key piece. How could it be? I'd seen Blackburn destroy it. But my fingers recognized the piece at once. With the necklace gripped tight in my fist, I swam for the dock. As soon as my hands touched wood, I pulled myself up and felt inside my coat for the key. At first I couldn't find it and I was sure I must have lost it in the water. Then I discovered it jammed into a corner of my coat pocket.

I turned to look at Jennie. She was still up, but her face was white and her lips were turning blue. "Hold on!" I called.

"I'm trying." Her voice was weak and her arms were moving slower. As I watched, she dipped below the surface and came up hacking.

With hands that were numb and trembling, I struggled to open the clasp of the necklace; my fingers felt slow and stupid.

"I can't do it," Jennie cried, and I turned to see her slip under the water again.

For a second I thought she was going to stay down. I held

my breath, watching. Then her water-darkened hair burst above the water and we both gasped for air at the same time.

"Can't . . ."

"Don't give up!" She couldn't die. Not when I was so close to saving her.

Once I got the piece off the chain, I still had to take apart the key and put the pieces back in the right order. My head was pounding. The pieces all looked the same. I couldn't seem to get them onto the rod again. One fell to the dock and I grabbed it just before it tumbled into the water.

I was starting to lose hope when the last piece clicked in place.

"Got it!" I looked out over the water, holding up the key.

But Jennie was gone.

I searched the pond, praying for her to rise one last time. *One thousand one . . . one thousand two.* She wasn't coming up.

"Please, Heavenly Father. Don't let her drown!" I leaped into the water and swam for the last place I'd seen her. My searching hands found nothing. *Down,* I realized. She must have sunk. Stroking and kicking, I propelled myself to the bottom of the pond. My reaching fingers slammed into the mud.

Where was she?

Grabbing at weeds and rocks, I pulled myself across the bottom. My right hand hit something solid. The anvil. I followed the chain until I found her unmoving body. Grabbing her face, I pressed my lips to hers and breathed out the last of my air. Was it enough? I didn't know, but I couldn't stay to find out. I followed the chain. My chest was burning. Black dots floated in front of my eyes, but I couldn't give up. My hands found the lock. I tried to put the key in, but my fingers wouldn't obey my commands. The hole felt too small, the key the wrong size. I couldn't do it. The key started to slip away from me as I felt a hand close over mine.

Unable to hold my breath any longer, I opened my mouth and cold, dirty water poured down my throat and into my lungs. My hand fell open. My head floated back. It was too late. I'd failed.

It's crazy how you think you know what's important in life. You think you've got it all figured out. Then something slams into you from out of the blue and you find yourself looking at life in a whole new way. Your priorities are flipped upside down. It's enough to make you suspect that us teenagers don't know everything after all—almost.

CHAPTER 24

I woke to the sound of someone sobbing hysterically nearby. A moment later, I made out Jennie's voice. "No, Father. Please . . . don't do . . . this."

Why was her father here? Did he want to finish what he'd started behind his blacksmith shop? I tried to get up, but was too weak. I rolled onto my side and water gushed from my mouth. Coughing and gagging, I forced my eyes open.

Jennie was on her knees about ten feet away, facing the other direction. She was soaking wet. Her dress was covered with moss from the pond and torn in several places. Her bonnet was gone, and her dripping hair clung to her face and neck. Crying so hard that her body shook, she hadn't heard me wake up. I looked for Mr. Jagger, but she and I were the only ones in sight. There was no one anywhere near the pond and the cabin looked deserted.

"Don't let him . . . be . . . dead." Jennie gasped the words out between her tears.

I realized it wasn't Mr. Jagger she was talking to. It was her Father in Heaven. She was praying—praying for me. I got to my hands and knees and crawled across the damp grass where, what could only have been a few minutes before, I had wondered if I had caused her death.

I reached out and touched her shoulder. "Jennie, I'm—"

My words were cut off as Jennie spun around and gave a scream that could probably have been heard all the way back in Utah. Her mouth flew open and her eyes went so wide I thought she was going to jump to her feet and run into the woods. She didn't run though. Instead she drove straight at me like a linebacker making a game-saving tackle. Her arms wrapped around my neck and her wet hair slapped me in the face.

"You're not dead!" she shrieked, hugging me until I could hardly breathe.

"Not yet," I said, tugging her hair out of my mouth. "But I can't promise anything if you keep squeezing me like this."

"I'm sorry." She pulled back, tears in her eyes. But a second later she was squeezing me again. I have to admit, I really didn't mind.

"After I opened the lock, I pulled you out of the water. But you weren't breathing," she said, her cheek pressed against mine so tightly I could feel the heat of her face on my cold skin. "I tried to wake you up, but you wouldn't move. Your skin was white and clammy. Your lips were blue. I was sure . . ."

She grabbed my shoulders and pushed me away, studying me as if making sure I was really alive. Then she did something I totally didn't expect. She took my face in both hands and before I could say a word, she pulled me toward her and kissed me.

I'm not going to say I hadn't kissed a girl before. But I will say that none of the previous kisses were anything compared to the kiss Jennie gave me on the edge of that pond, both of us wet from head to foot and nearly freezing in the cold morning air. If all the other kisses in my life combined together were a candle, this was a flamethrower. No concussion had ever left me more dazed.

"Whoa," I managed when I could finally catch my breath.

Her face was bright red, but she didn't let go of me, clinging to my hand like I was a balloon she was afraid might float away. "I still can barely believe you're alive," she said. "You weren't breathing for so long. I was sure . . ." Her voice trailed off and her gaze dropped to her hands.

"It must have been the Fourth Nephite thing," I said. I'd wondered if it went as far as protecting me from death. Now I knew. I looked toward the pond, and a chill shook my body as I remembered I wasn't the only one who'd come close to dying.

"How did you do it?" I asked. "I saw Blackburn destroy the last part to the key. How did you get it?"

The flecks of green in her eyes gleamed as she grinned. "My father's a blacksmith."

It took me a moment to grasp the meaning of her words. Then I couldn't help myself from laughing out loud. "You made a copy?"

She nodded. "After we talked outside the church, I was sure you couldn't be the kind of person my father thought you were. I knew he had the letter, and I had a pretty good idea it was for you. But I didn't know how important it was until we talked the next day. By that time I'd taken the letter. I knew I should give it to you, but I was afraid what my father would do if he found out. And . . ."

She looked down at her hands which were still gripping mine tightly. "After I realized what my father had done to you, I was afraid he would destroy the letter and what was inside. I used his tools to make a copy of the key piece and replaced the pendant on my necklace with it. I was on my way back to the house when those men caught me. I know I should have given it to you before, but I was afraid that once you had it, you'd leave."

"Well, I guess we don't have to worry about that anymore." I stared at the pond and sighed. "We'll never find it at the bottom of that."

Jennie released my fingers with one of her hands, before pressing something cold and hard against my palm. I looked down.

It was the key.

□   □   □

"Is there really a door?" Jennie concentrated on the side of the hill where I knew she could see only tall grass and dirt.

I nodded. The air had dried most of the moisture from our wet clothes and hair as we walked back to the spot where it had all begun, but we still looked like a couple of bedraggled rats. I fingered the key.

"Once you go through, it will disappear, won't it?" she asked.

"I don't know," I said. But I had a pretty good idea. This door had been created for me. Maybe it would go away once I went through it. Or maybe it would just move somewhere else, waiting for the next person who had a lesson to learn—a journey to take. But whether or not it stayed, with the key gone, it would be unusable.

Jennie stepped forward and grabbed my hand the way she had done at the pond. "Take me with you!"

I looked into her eyes and knew I would have done anything she asked me to if it was in my power—anything except for what she was asking. "I don't know if it would work—if you could even go through the door. And if you could, you wouldn't be able to come back. You'd leave your family. You'd change your future." Something about that gave me a weird feeling inside, like there was something I should remember, only I couldn't quite figure out what it was.

"I guess I could stay here," I said. It really wasn't a bad place, and I supposed I could get used to outhouses and chamber pots. But Jennie was shaking her head before the words finished leaving my mouth.

"You have a family to return to. They must be terribly worried."

At the thought of my mom and dad—and all my crazy brothers—I felt a pull in my stomach. I couldn't stay. And she couldn't come with me. I drew her into my arms. "I'll never forget you," I whispered.

She pulled out of my embrace and stepped back. "Go," she said, wiping tears from her eyes. "The longer you stay, the harder this is going to be."

I knew she was right and still I wanted to turn back—to stay just another day or two. Instead I pushed the key into the lock and twisted it. A whoosh of warm air blew through my hair, and a strange golden light filtered through the cracks.

"I saw it!" Jennie cried. "For just a minute, I saw the door."

I turned to see her beaming face, and again something tugged at my memory. Something about her eyes—the way she almost glowed when she smiled. The door began to swing open, and the air around me rippled. The trees, the grass, even the sun started to fade. Jennie was fading too. She raised her hand, and all at once I remembered. The first time I'd seen her, I'd thought she looked familiar—like I'd seen her before. I hadn't seen *her*, but I'd seen someone who looked just like her. Someone who could have been a relative, a distant relative.

The door was more than halfway open now, and I found I could read the letters on the inside. Knowledge and faith. Of course. Words came back to me—words I'd heard in what seemed like years before: "My great-great-great grandmother's great-great-grandmother was one of the earliest members of the Church."

Jennie was the person the girl in the shop had been talking about. Jennie was supposed to join the Church. I had to tell her. I tried to step away from the door, but it was pulling me in. Jennie was a single point of light in a tunnel of darkness that was quickly closing around her. The warm breeze had turned into a gale, tearing me away.

"Joseph Smith!" I yelled. "He really is a prophet." The wind roared in my ears, yanking my words away as quickly as I spoke them.

Jennie cupped her hands to the side of her head, her face questioning. She yelled something back, but I couldn't hear what she was saying.

"Talk to him!" I screamed. Why hadn't I told her earlier? Why hadn't I borne my testimony when I had the chance? "Read the Book of Mormon. It's true. It *is* the word of God."

"Is that right?" a gruff voice said.

The light changed and I found myself standing in front of a counter in a small, dimly lit room. I was back in Ladan's office that was filled with shelves and shelves of books. I spun around, but Jennie was gone. It was too late.

"Sounds like you've had quite a change of heart."

I turned to see Ladan watching me with his strange silvery eyes.

"I didn't get a chance to bear my testimony to her," I said. "I tried to, but I'm not sure she heard me."

He smiled gently. "It can be frustrating when those who cannot hear our words are the ones who need them most."

I knew he wasn't talking about Jennie. "I thought I knew a lot more than I did."

"You are a teenager."

"Is she . . . Is Jennie going to join the Church?"

He shrugged and began sorting through a handful of

books. "No one can make anyone do anything. All we can do is share what we know and hope our words get through."

I thought about what I knew. About how I'd seen the plates, touched them. About the words Joseph had spoken to me in the living room of his parents' house and out in the field. I thought about the fortune-teller, Alistair Bascom. But that wasn't right, was it? His last name wasn't Bascom. It was . . . I searched my mind but I couldn't remember. I remembered he'd had a mustache . . . or had it been a beard? I tried to remember whether we'd met in a cabin . . . or an inn.

Things were fading. I'd had dinner with the Smiths, or had it been lunch? Had Joseph thrown a roll or whacked one of his brothers with a spoon? Desperately I tried to remember how the golden plates had looked—how heavy they'd been in my hands. But it was all disappearing.

"Is there a problem?" Ladan asked, somehow sensing my distress.

"I'm supposed to be a witness," I cried, trying to hold onto my memories, which were disappearing one by one. "Isn't that why you sent me back?"

Ladan smiled.

"I want to tell Jeff and the rest of my friends what I saw. I want to tell them it's all real. But how can I if I don't remember any of it?"

"How do you feel in your heart?" Ladan asked.

I tried to let go of my fear and listen to what he was asking.

"Good," I said after a moment. "I feel good in my heart— comforted."

"Men quickly forget what they've experienced. What is stored here." Ladan tapped the side of his head. "Laman and Lemuel witnessed an angel as they were beating their brother. But a few moments later, they doubted whether God could deliver the brass plates into their hands." He patted his chest. "What is stored here never goes away unless you let it. Your friends don't need to hear about what you saw. They need to hear about what you *know*."

"My testimony."

He chuckled. "There may be hope for you after all."

I glanced down at myself and for the first time realized I was somehow back in my old clothes again. I patted my pocket and was relieved to feel my cell phone.

"You may want to call your mother," Ladan said. "I phoned her and said you were with me, but that you might be home a little late."

"A *little?*" I grimaced at the thought of how worried and upset my parents would be. "Try four days. Or was it five?"

"You really are confused." Ladan put the books he'd been sorting on a nearby shelf. "We've been talking for only a half hour or so."

I checked my watch. He was right. It was still Friday, and it wasn't even ten o'clock yet. Something occurred to me. "Just now, when I patted my pocket, you knew I was checking for my cell phone. Did you hear me or can you see?"

"I see what I need to."

"Will we ever meet again?"

He shrugged. Another non-answer. "What do you think?"

I shrugged back. Let him make of that what he wanted.

He reached under the counter and pulled out a folded piece of paper. My name was printed on the outside in the spiky handwriting I recognized immediately. "I guess you'll be wanting this," he said with a gleam in his silvery eyes. "To show your seminary teacher you were here."

I grinned and shoved my hands deep into my coat pockets. "I don't think I'll be needing it anymore. I've got a big game to miss."

EPILOGUE

S he sat in the front seat of an immaculately recreated covered wagon and watched the boy exit the elevator. As he picked his way through the maze of historical odds and ends, she wondered if Ladan had been successful in helping him find the truth. There *did* seem to be something different about him now—an indefinable change in the way he walked, the way he tilted his head as he examined a blue-and-pink-flowered chamber pot with a wry grin and paused to run his fingers across the arm of a hand-carved rocking chair.

When he first entered the shop, he hadn't been full of himself like a lot of guys his age. In fact—if she was going to be perfectly honest with herself, which she liked to be whenever possible—he'd seemed sort of nice. And, okay, cute too. But he'd also seemed cocky—like he knew everything there was to know and was waiting for the rest of the world to catch up with him. The attitude probably made him good in sports, but it also left him vulnerable to the wrong influences.

It was hard to tell in the shadowy warehouse, but she thought that cockiness had been replaced by something even more powerful—confidence. She was good at reading people— it was one of the reasons Ladan had asked her to work for him—and she thought she sensed an inner strength in this boy that hadn't been there before.

He glanced at his watch and hurried to the front door, but before he reached to open it, he turned and stared into the dark building as though he was searching for something.

"You should go talk to him." The whisper that came to her ear was so close to her own thoughts that she jumped a little, thinking she'd spoken out loud. Then she turned to see Ladan's silvery eyes and his gentle—if slightly amused—smile.

"No. I couldn't. It's late. I have to get home. So does he."

The boy scanned the interior of the warehouse a few seconds longer, before turning with a shrug and walking into the alley.

"Did it work?" she asked. "Did he find what he needed to?"

Ladan climbed into the wagon and sat next to her. "What do *you* think?"

She pursed her lips and nodded. "I think he did." As she thought about what he must have seen, the experiences he must have had, the people he'd met, a hot flicker of jealousy burned in her chest. "Why can't I go? Just for a day."

Ladan patted her on the shoulder. "The door only appears for those who need it. You could spend hours searching those hallways and find nothing but cobwebs. And possibly a few books. I could swear the tunnels eat the exact volumes I'm looking for."

She sighed. He was right, of course. But still, after spending so much time studying history, learning everything she could about the amazing people who'd helped restore the gospel, it seemed incredibly unfair that she couldn't go back in time and see it for herself.

"So he doesn't need the door anymore."

"No."

She played with the bonnet in her lap, folding and refolding the stiff cloth. Like the door, this shop and the alleyway that connected it to the outside world only appeared for those who had a pressing need to find it. "I guess we won't see him again."

Ladan chuckled. "On the contrary, I believe he *will* be back."

Her heart thudded in a not-unpleasant kind of way. "But if he doesn't need to go through the door . . ."

"It won't be for him. He'll be back with a friend who requires the door even more than he did. And it could be much sooner than you think."

AUTHOR NOTES

I f you've just finished reading *The Fourth Nephite*, thanks! I hope you liked it half as much as I liked writing it. If you jumped to the back of the book before reading the story, shame on you! Go back and finish the story before I accidently reveal a plot point that will not only ruin the story for you, but will also cause you to break out in hives the size of tennis balls. (Okay, you may not get hives. But go back to the beginning anyway.)

Shortly after I began writing *The Fourth Nephite*, I came across a story about how most people think clothing worn hundreds of years ago was drab and boring. It's not the clothes themselves that were dull—in fact, many of the fabrics and colors used then were more vibrant and showy than those typically worn today—but because the clothes shown in museums have faded with time and age. When we see recreations of what outfits really looked like when they were originally worn, they come alive.

By writing this book I hope to give you, my readers, a glimpse of what it would be like to travel back in time, to bring alive people like Joseph Smith, Emma, Hyrum, and many of the colorful characters that lived in Palmyra during the early and mid-1800s.

Of course this story is also fiction. As far as I'm aware, no one has ever been sent back in time by one of the Three Nephites. Because this is a novel, it means I had to combine things that really happened and people who really lived with fictional characters who exist only in my mind (and after you read about them, in your mind as well). If you don't care about what is real and what I made up, you can close this book now and I promise not to think any less of you. But for those of you who are interested, here are some fun facts about *The Fourth Nephite*.

- Many of the minor characters in the book are real. Dr. Gain Robinson was one of several doctors who treated the Smith family. The story of the petition he drew up to help the Smith family—and the sixty signatures it received—is historically accurate. Major Obadiah Dickerson was the first postmaster of Palmyra, and he really did keep letters and important papers in his bell-crown hat.

- Pastor Wooster was the minister of the Palmyra congregation. I don't know for sure that he was the pastor at the time of this story, but it is quite likely. Before Joseph Smith had his vision in the Sacred Grove, he spent a great deal of time exploring the Methodist faith. For this reason, he went to the local Methodist minister after his vision. The minister didn't believe him, and Joseph was hurt and disappointed by the minister's response to his story.

- Many of the names I chose—including the Jagger family—came from lists of actual Palmyra families at the time.

- In 1824, the proprietors of Phelps Tavern enlarged it to three stories and named it The Eagle Hotel. It was the only three-story building in the village at the time (Richard L. Bushman, *Joseph Smith and the Beginnings of Mormonism* [Urbana: University of Illinois Press, 1984], 46).

- While there are tunnels under Salt Lake City, I'm pretty sure none of them lead back in time.

- Joseph describes the plates as having "the appearance of gold," being about six inches by eight inches by six inches (or 288 cubic inches in size), and having a surface engraved with figures of "curious workmanship." While we don't know one way or the other, it is likely the gold plates were not made of pure gold but some gold alloy that would have been both lighter and more durable than pure gold. Witnesses who held the plates said they weighed between forty and sixty pounds.

- Brigham Young stated that ten to twelve men working with Willard Chase hired a man to help them acquire the plates: "The man I refer to was a fortune-teller, a necromancer, an astrologer, a soothsayer, and possessed as much talent as any man that walked on the American soil, and was one of the wickedest men I ever saw" (in *Journal of Discourses,* 26 vols. [Liverpool: Latter-day Saints' Book Depot, 1854–86), 2:181). I made up the name Alistair Blackburn.

• Sally Chase claimed her green "peep stone" helped her locate hidden treasures, including the gold plates. Although these men and women were never able to obtain the plates, Joseph was warned that if he was not vigilant, the plates would be lost. The incident where Joseph and his family hid the plates in the fireplace hearth and then scared off armed men by shouting and pretending to be a bigger group actually happened (Lucy Mack Smith, *Biographical Sketches of Joseph Smith the Prophet and His Progenitors for Many Generations* [Liverpool: Published for O. Pratt, by S.W. Richards, 1853], 109).

• Joseph also buried the box containing the plates beneath the floor of the family cabin that had been converted into a cooper shop. He hid the plates in a loft above, covered by flax. In the morning, the floorboards were torn up, but the plates were not discovered (Lucy Mack Smith, *Biographical Sketches of Joseph Smith the Prophet and His Progenitors for Many Generations* [Liverpool: Published for O. Pratt, by S.W. Richards, 1853], 108–9).

- Although I made up the scene where Joseph Smith threw a roll across the table and tickled his little sister, there is ample evidence that Joseph loved to joke with his family and friends and enjoyed games of all types. Joseph often gathered his family around him to teach them religious concepts. The quotes I attribute to him in the living room of the Smith house and the next day in the field are taken directly from his later writings. The only changes I made were minor changes to things like tense or person.

- Kaleo, Jennie, Ladan, and the (as yet) unnamed girl who works with Ladan are figments of my imagination.

- The Three Nephites are real.

- Joseph Smith was a Prophet of God.